Women Drinking Benedictine

T0158287

Also by Sharon Dilworth

The Long White

WOMEN
DRINKING
BENEDICTINE

Sharon Dilworth

OHIO STATE UNIVERSITY PRESS

Columbus

Copyright © 1998 by The Ohio State University.
All rights reserved.

Library of Congress Cataloging-in-Publication Data

Dilworth, Sharon.
  Women drinking benedictine / Sharon Dilworth.
  p.   cm.
  ISBN 0-8142-5012-2 (pbk. : alk. paper)
  I. Title.
  PS3554.1436W6   1998
  813'.54—dc21   98-26156
                                                      CIP

Text and cover design by Gary Gore.
Type set in Adobe Garamond by G & S Typesetters, Inc.
Printed by Thomson-Shore, Inc.

The paper used in this publication meets the minimum requirements of the
American National Standard for Information Sciences—Permanence of
Paper for Printed Library Materials. ANSI Z39.48-1992.

9   8   7   6   5   4   3   2

The stories in this collection were originally published in the following:

Press: "Three Fat Women of (Pittsburgh Just Visiting) Antibes"
New Letters: "Women Drinking Benedictine"
Alaska Quarterly Review: "We're in Meadville"
Red Rock Review: "Me and Danno Booking 'Em Good"
River Styx: "Figures on the Shore"
River City Review: "This Month of Charity"
High Plains Literary Review: "Awaken with My Mother's Dreams"

The author is grateful to Carnegie Mellon University and the Virginia Center for the Creative Arts for their generous support. And for ever-faithful friends—Gerry Costanzo, Mathilde Doubinsky, Keya Ganguly, Marty Karabees, Tim Haggerty, Chuck Kinder. And for Jim Zafris, who helped Nancy find the towel hanging on the fence in Rigny Usse.

For Dogger and Dudley,
Kathleen, Mary, EJ III, and
for Dusty, always

Contents

Keeping the Wolves at Bay

THE SHOES WERE SO EUROPEAN. THE SLEEK black leather, the single side buckle, the sharp— but not too pointed—curve of the toe gave them a look that promised they would never be sold in the States, not even in L.A. Everyone was wearing them, and Steve did not want to go home without a pair. Still, he was cheap and cautious about spending money for something he wanted but did not need.

He and Max were in Nice, walking through the large and crowded flower market, when Steve spotted them on a distinguished-looking gray-haired man. "They are so sharp-looking," Steve fretted. "Tell me how these people can afford them."

And without another word Max marched him into a shoe store and bought him a pair.

"You can't do this," Steve protested. The store was on the rue Paradis, across from the Louis Vuitton and Coco Chanel shops.

It was elegant, the kind of place where tourists might press their noses to the glass, but would not dare enter.

"Nonsense," Max said in that sarcastic tone that puzzled Steve. "I can do anything I want."

The shoes were tight, but the salesman insisted they were a perfect fit. "Good leather will stretch to the length and width of the individual foot."

"The shoe that fits one person pinches another," Max said. "Just as there is no recipe for living that suits everyone."

Steve motioned for Max to wipe the tomato stain off his collar.

"Jung?" the salesman asked, and Max smiled.

"Very good." Max slid his Visa card across the counter, and Steve shook his hand in gratitude. "Thanks," he said. "When I wear them I'll think of you." They were expensive, but he was not going to feel guilty. He had been good company for Max. He had done what he had promised himself he would do.

"Oh God, I hope not," Max said. "Don't think of me. Think of someone you love."

Instead Steve thought that the shoes were going to look great with just about everything he owned.

Steve's two-week trek in France had been long, but not as dull as he'd imagined. He had gone as a favor to his father, who, before his death, had asked Steve to keep an eye on Max. "Make sure he's not lonely," his father directed. Max had been his dad's companion for twelve years, and he worried about how Max would manage once he was gone. Steve lived in Pittsburgh. His father and Max were in Detroit. He told his father keeping Max company might prove difficult.

"Do your best," his father said. "That's all I ask."

Steve's father thought it natural that Steve would continue to be a part of Max's life. Steve did not see this happening.

Steve tried to turn his father's wish into a joke. "Listen to you. You sound like a Christian martyr."

"I don't care if I sound like the Almighty Himself," his father agreed. "Do me this favor. Do it in memory of me."

Steve had made the sign of the cross, but his father had closed his eyes and was asleep before Steve could agree to anything.

Steve had never been comfortable with his father's homosexuality. It had not been the reason for his parent's divorce. No, there had been other problems there—mostly his mother's disregard for anyone who loved her—but still, Steve could not help feeling that his father's relationship with Max had cheated him. It wasn't fair that his father lived with a man. Steve would have preferred to ignore the sexual aspect of his father's life, but Max made that impossible. He did not want to see Max mourning after his father's death. He was not comfortable with talk about love. He did not like the term "soul mate."

The trip to France had been Max's idea. Steve agreed to it with a great deal of trepidation. He thought it might rid him of the dark shadow that had settled on his life since his father's death, but he worried about traveling with Max. They had never been particularly close, and Steve did not imagine them suddenly becoming friends.

But Max was a good traveling partner. Steve had no complaints there. Max was generous, pleasant, and for the most part, interesting. He could decipher maps. He was excellent with money and numbers and could translate the exchange rate in his head. He was fluent in French, spoke some Italian, and had enough Spanish to read a menu.

Max was a good conversationalist and was endlessly entertaining during the long French meals that started with cocktails, moved to wine, then finished hours later with coffee.

"You should have written for Hollywood," Steve told him one night.

"These are just boring stories about my life," Max said. "They wouldn't interest anybody."

"I don't know about that," Steve said. The wine made him enthusiastic. Steve was aware of Max's attitude, which was slightly condescending. It suggested, at least to Steve, that he was angry about the way Steve had treated him all these years. Steve did not want to bring it up, but it was there, a slight bitterness that he could not ignore no matter how pleasant Max acted.

"How about we do this again?" Max asked Steve. They had just spent the day in the Pyrenees, and Steve thought he wanted to go back to Spain.

"No, no, no. I meant how about another two weeks in Europe?" Max said. "We seem to travel well together. I wouldn't mind checking out northern Italy if you can spare the time."

"I'd love to," Steve said. "But I can't. I'm getting married."

"That's right. You mentioned that a number of times," Max said, and then he smirked. "I hope you're going to invite me to your wedding."

"Of course," Steve said. "Why wouldn't I invite you?"

The reason he wasn't going to invite him was that he had not told his fiancée the truth about Max. He had identified Max as an older relative—a rich uncle who did not care to travel alone. Kathleen, in fact, knew very little about his father. Steve thought it best that things had worked out the way they had. She was not a warm person. In fact in the last couple of months, she had become difficult, almost bitchy. Steve could not help but feel her anger was directed at him, as if perhaps she didn't like him as much as he liked her. He could not imagine her understanding the Max situation.

"If I can't make it I'll send an objet d'art," Max said. "A faux objet d'art."

"Fine," Steve said. He sensed that Max was mocking him, but he was not sure. It was not like Max to make fun of something like marriage. Steve unfolded the road map as a way to change the subject.

"I'll send something that's unbelievably ugly. An outrageous piece of contemporary sculpture. It will be heavy and awkward and every time you move, you'll curse the damn relative who gave it to you."

Steve nodded. "That would be great."

"Seriously," Max said and raised his glass. "Here's to love. May it come along at least once in your life."

"Yes," Steve said, wishing Max would lower his voice.

"Here's to not getting cold feet at the last minute," Max said and stood, moving his chair away from the table. "Don't run from love. No matter how afraid you are of it."

"I've got my new shoes," Steve said. "How cold could my feet get?"

Max did not reply. He stopped the waiter and paid with three or four large colorful French bills, and for a moment Steve felt like a child at a grown-up dinner party.

Max was incredibly knowledgeable about the religious history of the southwest part of France, and this was where he wanted to spend most of their time. He thought it would be interesting to follow the path the Cathars took in the 1200s when they traveled the area trying to avoid the tyranny of the Catholic Church. He gave Steve short lectures before they visited each town.

"Don't tell me you spent the winter months with your head in a bunch of boring books memorizing this stuff," Steve said. They had talked infrequently since his father's death. It was usually Max calling and leaving a message, then Steve returning his call during the day when he knew Max would be at work. They had worked out the itinerary for the trip this way.

"Oh no," Max said. "I'm quite familiar with this history. You'd be surprised how interesting the Cathars were."

Steve had never heard of them, and therefore judged them an unnecessary part of foreign history—nothing at all to do with him. He ignored Max's lectures and complained about the mildewy odor and dampness of the cathedrals.

Max's enthusiasm did not wane with Steve's dismissal of and disdain for the area.

"The Cathars were a fascinating people who were faulted because they opposed the Catholic Church. They found its ways corrupt, which in the thirteenth century was true. They were essentially a nonviolent people who took refuge in these towns."

Visiting ruined castles in a series of look-alike medieval towns was not Steve's idea of a vacation, and he complained often of boredom.

Max remained cheerful. "This stuff is stunning history," he said as they drove into the town of Monségur one morning.

A wave of self-pity washed over Steve. He wished he were back in Pittsburgh. He and his fiancée had been fighting, and he had been glad for the time away, but the trip was long and being with Max was getting tiresome.

Steve parked in the town square and the two of them walked toward the cathedral. An albino beggar stood outside the wooden doors, his hands cupped waiting for spare change. Steve was sure they had seen the same man in the town they toured the day before.

"I'll wait out here for you," Steve said.

"Are you sure you want to miss this one?" Max said. "It's a biggie."

Steve told him he'd be in the town center, sleeping in the shade of the elm trees.

"I might be a while," Max said. He had loaded a new roll of film and wore his camera around his neck like a piece of jewelry.

"Take your time," Steve said.

Across the way a trio of men played *boules*. They argued loudly, debating every shot, and the game moved slowly.

The day was warm and Steve took off his sweater and closed his eyes in the sunshine.

Steve slept. He woke when the church bells rang noon. He got up to tell Max it was time for lunch.

Max was on the altar, explaining the enormous frescoes to a trio of heavyset American women who seemed delighted to find someone who not only spoke English but was also informative.

Max was in his glory. "In 1244, after a long siege, the surviving leader of the Cathar church surrendered. Given a choice of renouncing their faith or being burned at the stake, two hundred men and women serenely climbed onto their funeral pyres."

"How do you know they went serenely?" Steve interrupted.

The women, full of eager and curious smiles, turned to look at him as if he were a zoo animal.

"Who's to say they weren't scared shitless?" Steve asked.

Max did not miss a beat. "And this pleasant young man is my friend, Steven."

Steve scowled. He did not like Max to introduce him in this way, lest people mistake him for something he was not. But these women were in their sixties—they wore large shapeless sweaters, brightly colored stretch pants, and sensible walking shoes. Loud, obviously American, they were not of sufficient attractiveness for Steve to care what they thought of him.

The women offered to buy Max lunch in exchange for the history lesson, and Max graciously accepted for the two of them.

"I wasn't expecting a crowd today," Steve complained to Max. The church gave him the creeps, and he walked down the aisle quickly, trying to hurry Max out of the cavelike structure.

"A little company might cheer you up." Max stopped at the back of the church and lit a candle. The money box had been left open. It was empty, but Max put a ten-franc coin in.

"Big spender," Steve said.

"In memory of your father," Max said.

Steve stepped outside and shivered in the bright sunlight.

The only restaurant in town was slightly crowded. The owner led them to the table smack-dab in the center of everyone's curious glances. Steve knew their loud American voices would soon fill the small room. They would be on display, like goldfish in a glass bowl.

The women were obviously flattered by Max's attention. They giggled through his wine order and asked him for lunch suggestions.

"It's such a relief not to struggle with the language," they said. They got giddy after the appetizer plate and demanded that Max continue his lecture on the Cathars.

"You're so eloquent," one remarked. She had her pen out and was writing furiously on her napkin. The napkin was a dark shade of blue, the same color as the ink. Steve looked over and could not see any of the words she wrote. Still, she scribbled furiously, as if she would be tested on it the next day.

"They believed in the rival energies of Good and Evil. Lightness and darkness were their guides," Max explained. Steve finished his third glass of wine. He tipped the bottle over to show Max that it was empty, and Max motioned for the waiter to bring another to the table. Max, the perfect host, did not skimp when it came to the palate.

"The Cathars were not happy with life. They found it terrifying—the ultimate punishment that God could inflict on a people. Birth was a misfortune. Death was a deliverance," Max said.

"I know exactly how they felt," Steve said loudly.

"My friend isn't interested in history," Max explained. "He enjoys being the center of attention, which is difficult when you're talking about the thirteenth century."

"How can you not find all this fascinating?" The largest woman leaned across the table and held onto Steve's wrist. He prodded her with his fork, then excused himself as if it had been an accident.

"What's not to like?" another of the women asked. She was scowling as if it had never occurred not to like what so many others admired.

"I'm of the mindset, you've seen one old church, you've seen them all," Steve said. "I mean, really, what's the point?"

His remark changed the mood of the meal, and the women finished their lunch with the insistence that they had someplace to be that afternoon. They did not stay for coffee.

Max was disappointed, and after the women left, he called Steve a spoilsport.

"I'm used to your temper tantrums," he said. The two of them walked outside. "But you could have been nice to them. They were interesting and kind. You didn't have to ruin their lunch."

"I was just stating my opinion," Steve said. "That's not a crime, is it?"

"Your opinion?" Max asked. He picked up a stone and tossed it toward the large oak tree in the center of town. A trio of squirrels scattered with the noise.

Steve felt he had to explain himself. "This place is just so depressing."

"To you," Max said. "But obviously not to those women. We were having a nice lunch. You were being rude."

"They were boring," Steve said.

"You mean I was boring," Max said.

"It's just boring here," Steve said. "It's dull as death."

Max threw another stone at the tree. The squirrels were gone, and the stone missed the target by six or seven feet.

Steve had every reason to complain. Except for the miles of sunflower fields, the whole area was gray and lifeless. The churches were exactly the same. There was nothing to look at but old men bowling under the trees.

"You win," Max said and dropped his hands. The remaining stones fell around their feet. "I give up."

Max took him to the Côte d'Azur. The few cathedrals in the resort towns were filled with chandeliers, glass jewels, warm-colored drapes, richly painted statues, brightly stained glass windows. Nothing smelled.

The sun was shining on the Mediterranean. The beaches were jammed. The breezes were warm—the surf a beautiful hue of blue. The streets were filled with noisy, honking tourists. The souvenir shops were spilling over with shoppers. The cafes were crowded, and the lines at the museums snaked around the block—the wait was at least an hour. Max was miserable, but Steve's spirits lifted immediately.

"Come on," Steve said. "Isn't this better?"

"For you," Max agreed. "Maybe this will put an end to your whining."

Until they got to the Riviera, Steve and Max had avoided any long talk about Steve's father. But after their visit to the shoe store, they walked to the beach and sat at a boardwalk cafe. The Mediterranean was a wild shade of blue-green, and they abandoned plans to drive the mountain roads in favor of drinking beer in the sun. Apropos of nothing, Max told Steve how much he missed Carl.

Steve turned away. He did not want to have this conversation.

Max borrowed a cigarette from the young woman at the next table, apologizing profusely. Ten minutes later he asked for another, then another. Finally, she threw the pack of cigarettes at him.

"I'm so sorry," Max said, upset that he had made the woman angry.

"Next time buy your own," she snarled in English, and then took some francs off their table.

Max lit a cigarette. Tears ran down his cheeks. "Your father was the greatest," Max said. "I just think you should know that your father was the greatest man who ever lived. I really miss him."

The cafe was jammed with tourists and Steve was certain that most of them spoke or at least understood English.

"Let's talk about something else," Steve said. His father had been dead six months and he was not ready to think about him. The cancer, which had started in his stomach, then spread to his lungs, had starved his father, leaving him unable to eat for the last three months of his life. "Let's have fun," Steve said. "There's no sense worrying about the past. We can't change anything that's already happened."

"I forgot, I forgot. I'm sorry," Max said. "Steve, Mr. Emotional Hologram, doesn't like to talk about personal things."

"Excuse me?" Steve said. He sobered almost immediately at the criticism.

"An emotional hologram," Max said and hiccuped. "That's what your father used to call you. Always best to stay a little bit shallow. Talk about the weather, books, some sports. But don't dig too deep."

Steve leaned on the table and stared out at the ocean. The sudden shift in weight tilted the table, and their beer mugs slid across the slick surface. He tried to catch them, which didn't help. Everything tipped at once. The glass smashed. The Americans across the way burst into applause—everyone else just stared. The waiter was there in a flash. He had already collected for their last round of beers. He offered Steve a police escort out of the cafe.

"It's not necessary," Steve said. "In fact, we were just leaving."

"There's just one thing I want to say." Max was still under the impression that they were having a conversation.

Steve pulled him down the boardwalk, where Max yelled his feelings to the ocean.

"I loved your father," Max said. "I really loved that man."

"Yes," Steve said. "I loved him, too." The sun had moved behind a cloud. The sea had changed color. He lifted his head, his hands stiff to keep himself from crying. He cleared his mind, deliberately not thinking of his father.

Max did not cry anymore on the trip, though he did buy a number of postcards, saying each time, "I wish I could mail this one to your father."

They spent Steve's last night in Paris.

All in all Steve was happy. He could go back to Pittsburgh

satisfied that he had made good on his father's request. It had not
been a perfect trip, but he had kept his promise to his father, and
that was what was important.

It was time to go home. In two months he would be married
and would not have to worry about spending time with his father's friend.

In his Paris hotel room, he took a cold shower, then, not
ready to dress for dinner, he found the cleanest pair of socks he
had and tried on his new shoes.

The only mirror in the room was over the bathroom sink.
He had to stand on the toilet to see himself. The shoes were
stylish. He would carry them on the plane and put them on
before getting off. There was always the threat of his feet
swelling, but he wanted to be wearing them when he first saw
Kathleen.

He looked up to see Max's reflection in the mirror.

"They look great," Max said.

"Jesus Christ," Steve shouted and jumped off the toilet. His
shoes slipped on the wet tiles and Max kept him from falling by
holding his elbow. Steve pulled away. He picked a towel off the
floor. It was damp from his shower and uncomfortable next to
his dry clean skin.

"Sorry," Max said. "I knocked lightly, but thought you might
be sleeping."

"Jesus Christ!" Steve yelled.

"I'm sorry," Max said. "I didn't mean to scare you."

Steve was not scared, but his heart was racing.

"Fuck it, Max," Steve said. "Can't a guy have a little privacy?
I've been with you for fourteen fucking days. Give me some
space."

"My fault. I didn't mean to be too familiar. I just think of you
as family. I didn't realize it was necessary to knock. Excuse me."

Max bowed, as if humbling himself. He left the room as quickly as he had entered.

"Wait," Steve said. "Max?" He opened the door. "Are you there, Max?"

The lights in the hall were on a timer, and they shut off, leaving the small space in darkness.

"I'm sorry, Max," Steve said and closed the door, certain that Max had heard his apology.

They walked the streets of the Latin Quarter, where three or four men called to them in English. "Eat here. Good and Cheap. Get a Fine French Meal."

Max seemed oblivious to the obvious tourist trappings of the area. He took no time deciding on a restaurant, simply choosing the first one. He pulled out a chair and motioned for Steve to sit across from him. "This okay?"

Steve did not want to argue.

They ordered the night's special and were served in a matter of minutes.

"High turnover seems to be the goal of the night," Steve said. "I've never seen waiters move so quickly." He would rather have been eating in a better quality place, where the waiters were rude, the food and drink pricey but delicious.

"Just as well," Max said. "I'm tired." It was the first time Steve had ever heard him complain. "I guess all this traveling has finally caught up with me."

"How about a walk along the Seine?" Steve said. He hadn't meant to lash out at him. A fight was a fight and then it was best to forget it ever happened. He had apologized—at least three times.

"You go," Max said. "I'm beat." He was planning to spend a week in Paris and then head into Italy. He would fly back to Detroit from Florence.

Steve had thought they would meet for breakfast, but Max turned to face him when they got to the hotel.

"You have a safe flight and call me to let me know when that wedding of yours is going to be." He held out his hand.

"I will," Steve promised and shook Max's hand a dozen times. "Listen. Thanks for everything. Everything. I mean it. It's been great. Just great."

"See you soon," Max said and disappeared into the dark entranceway of the hotel.

Steve should have been elated that the trip was almost over. He had done what his father had asked, and yet he couldn't help but feel that something was wrong.

He walked across the river and sat on the steps of Notre Dame. The summer crowd was dense and slightly unruly. A few kids offered to sell him pot. No one was speaking French. Not used to being alone, he left.

He was nervous and excited when he landed in Pittsburgh. He looked forward to seeing Kathleen. He was anxious to start planning their wedding. He did not want to think about Max. If Max was upset with him, that was his problem. Steve had done nothing wrong.

Kathleen told him he looked like he had grown.

"Grown?" he asked, hoping she was making a joke. He thought of all the beer he had been drinking, the late-night meals, the sugar and milk in the coffee. He didn't feel heavy, but he put his hand over his belt and pressed in his stomach.

"Taller," Kathleen clarified. "You look like you've grown a foot."

With that, Steve wondered if she had been unfaithful. She was obviously comparing him to the shorter man she had been sleeping with while he was away. He began to panic, then deliberately pushed these thoughts aside. He was tired—he had watched both movies on the plane and had not slept at all. He cleared his head and asked about the weather. "Has it been brutally hot?"

Kathleen grinned. "Is that what they're talking about in Europe nowadays? The weather?"

"Yes," Steve said. He was at once awkward and self-conscious. Kathleen was not a sarcastic person, and he felt himself on unsteady ground.

He knew what was coming.

Kathleen had been moody and sharp before he left, and he had thought that the time apart would do them some good. He had been wrong. She was even more moody and more sharp than before he left.

She was ruthless, breaking off their engagement on the highway. Steve, sitting in the passenger seat in her non-air-conditioned car, was sick as he listened to her speak.

Her reasons for the breakup were varied.

"I love you, but my feelings have changed," she explained. "I need some time. A wedding in October, come on. It's already August."

It was August, Steve thought. Hot, dry, vapid August, and I'm in Pittsburgh, Pennsylvania. His contacts were dry, his body dehydrated from the flight. Up ahead, he could see the flashing brake lights of the cars slowing down before they entered the Fort Pitt tunnels. The Pirates were playing at Three Rivers Stadium, and traffic came to a standstill just outside the city.

His car had been broken into. Why it was parked on the street instead of in the garage was hard for Kathleen to explain. Something to do with a friend not having a Shadyside parking permit.

"You could have cleaned up the glass," Steve said.

"I didn't think about it," Kathleen said with a shrug.

"I guess there's a lot you didn't think about," Steve snapped.

"I knew you were going to be a shit about this," Kathleen said. She had not even said a word about his tan, nothing at all about his new shoes—which were pinching his skin. He was sure to have blisters in the morning.

He was tired of talking to her and wanted her to go home. "I want the ring back," he said. He had been wrong about her. She was never going to make him happy.

"You're not supposed to ask for the ring back," she scolded.

"You broke off the engagement," Steve said. "I have every right to ask for my ring back. Consult Miss Manners."

There was one bottle of Heineken in the refrigerator, a few dried carrots, and a crushed carton of baking powder in the back corner. "It's mine and I want it back."

"Is that all you can say?" Kathleen asked. "What about your feelings? Aren't you upset that this is over?"

"The ring belonged to my mother. It's the only thing I have of hers," Steve lied. Kathleen was a tricky person. She was not above taking things that did not belong to her. He wanted it back.

"You never told me it was your mother's," Kathleen said.

His feet were numb, his skin unbelievably hot and prickly. He went to the bedroom, where she continued arguing.

He heard her voice as if it came over the radio, distant, not directed to him.

He flew back to Paris the next night. He saw no reason to be in Pittsburgh when news of his breakup got around—stupid questions, people trying to be nice. He would rather continue accompanying Max. A week in Italy would be nice. Using the frequent flier miles his father had willed him in his estate, the round-trip ticket cost him only $157.43. It was daring, and he felt cosmopolitan about crossing the ocean twice in two days.

It was not quite seven in the morning when the taxi dropped him off in front of Max's hotel.

The desk clerk recognized him. He, at least, smiled at Steve. "Bonjour, monsieur," he said.

"Mon ami est ici?" Steve asked, straining his French vocabulary.

"He is in room 513," the man answered in English. The hotel smelled of vinegar, just as Steve had remembered it. He was excited and took the steps two at a time. He knocked with force, anxious to see Max's face when he opened the door.

"Well," Max said. He was wearing nylon running shorts. They were neon green.

"Going for a jog?" Steve asked.

"What are you doing here?" Max asked.

"Surprised?" Steve asked.

"Very," Max agreed. "What are you doing here?"

It had been worth the long flight, Steve thought. They could drive to Italy, stop in some interesting places, and by the time he returned to Pittsburgh, he would have all but forgotten Kathleen. He could shrug off all questions about why their engagement had broken off.

"Did you miss your plane?" Max asked.

It was a stupid question and Steve smiled. "I reconsidered your offer for two weeks in Italy. It looks like I have the time after all."

Max did not say anything. He was not wearing shoes and his bare feet were pale in the harsh overhead light.

Steve smiled. The trip to Pittsburgh had been a waste of time. He should have called Kathleen and saved himself the trouble and expense of flying home. "Isn't it great? I can go with you to Italy."

Max looked at him carefully.

"Aren't you going to ask me in?" Steve asked.

Max looked over his shoulder, hesitating. He pulled the door toward him, and in this moment Steve understood that Max was not alone.

"I don't believe it," Steve said.

"Oh, Steve," Max said. He spoke with pity as if he felt sorry for Steve.

"There's someone in your room, isn't there?" Steve did not have to ask, but he wanted to hear Max admit it. "My father's been dead less than a year and you're with someone else."

Max hushed him.

"What about my father?" Steve said. "Does your new friend know about my father?"

"Of course not," Max said. "Lower your voice, please."

"You talk about me being an emotional hologram," Steve said. "You're an emotional zero."

"Let's go outside," Max suggested. "We can go for a walk."

"No," Steve said. He was furious. Betrayed. He had been gone less than forty-eight hours and Max had already found someone else to be with. "You make me sick," he yelled.

"Steve," Max said. There was no mistaking the condescension in his voice now. "We're both adults here. This has nothing to do with your father."

"I thought you were having a good time with me. Obviously not. The minute I leave, you find someone new to lecture about evil and good. You're a fine one to talk about evil. I just wonder what my father would feel about all this."

"Be quiet, Steve," Max said. "You don't know what you're talking about."

"Don't you try to deny it," Steve said. "Whatever you do, don't lie to me." People were always disappointing him. They never, never acted like he wanted them to.

"Let me get dressed," Max said. "Wait here while I put on some clothes. We can go down the street for coffee."

"Not with you," Steve yelled. "Absolutely not. I don't want to go anywhere with you ever again."

"Steve," Max started.

"Never," Steve yelled, and he continued yelling, even after Max slammed the door in his face. Even after the light timer switched off and the hall fell into complete darkness, even when the desk clerk threatened to call the police, when the tall woman in the room next door screamed that he was a lunatic, Steve yelled. The world was not treating him fairly, and he had every right to be pissed. Life owed him something, and that's all he wanted—just the things he should be getting, just the things he deserved.

Leather Goods

INNIE MARTIN WORKED IN A leather goods shop in the Shady-side neighborhood of Pittsburgh, Pennsylvania. She was an ill-informed retailer when it came to selling leather—fringed, spangled, painted, or tooled, it was all cowhide to her. Still, she was reliable, and when encouraged could be savvy, though not hip, about the merchandise she sold.

The owner of the store, a longtime friend of Winnie's, suggested Winnie describe the leather as "half Miami Beach–Jewish flea market—half Harley-biker-babe wear." Winnie would rather have died than follow Suzanne's advice. When people asked about the clothes, she simply said that most of the outfits did not flatter a woman her age. A fifty-three-year-old rear end did not look good tucked into skintight biker leather. Perhaps a tailored woolen skirt would be more appropriate. Talbots was right around the corner.

The owner was too busy to notice or care what Winnie said about the clothes. She had gotten married in December to a man who was determined to bring riverfront gambling to Pittsburgh. He envisioned the city as the next Las Vegas or Atlantic City, and they spent most of their time touring different casinos around the country—leaving Winnie to mind the cowhide.

"The Monongahela's a dream spot compared to some of the dismal places we've seen," Suzanne told her. She was making a pit stop in the Steel City before traveling on to northern Michigan. Her enthusiasm did not convince Winnie that Pittsburgh could ever become a tourist attraction. "Indian reservations are the worst," Suzanne continued as Winnie rearranged the pale leather bags in the front window. "Tacky, badly painted buildings. Cheap nickel slot machines. The weather is terrible. You end up spending half your time in tanning booths. And believe me, you don't know boring until you gamble at one of those places."

But boring was just how Winnie would have described Pittsburgh—it was a strange city that seemed to exist in a state where the more things stayed the same, the more things had to stay the same. The only thing that did change was the rents. They kept rising, making it difficult for private businesses to prosper. The chain stores were moving in everywhere, even on Walnut Street. The once trendy, funky street now looked like a suburban shopping mall. Winnie was not without hope, though. Maybe she was wrong. Maybe gambling would make the city a glamorous place to live.

Running the leather shop was dull. Of this, Winnie was certain. The heat was bad in the winter, the air conditioner stalled in the summer. Standing in the shop window, Winnie watched the seasons come and go. Whatever the weather, people went elsewhere to shop. The store seemed to reflect her own middle age: mostly alone, always dull.

Winnie spent most of her days reading. The corner bookstore flooded when the Ann Taylor shop expanded to the second story. The bookstore owner threw out a box full of Penguin Classics. Winnie rescued them before the garbage men could get to them. The books were mildewed and smelled of bug spray, but they still were readable. Hardy, Fielding, Strindberg—these were names she recognized but had never read. Winnie dried the books out in the microwave, which unglued the binding. She read a page, and when it broke away from the spine, she tossed it into the trash.

The bells above the door jingled against the glass—almost noon, the first customer of the day. Winnie wound a rubber band around *Far from the Madding Crowd*. She was not enjoying the book. Like in *Tom Jones*, the chapter titles gave away the plot. "Chapter VII—In Which the Lady Pays a Visit to Mr. Jones." "Chapter III—The arrival of Mr. Jones, with his Lady, at the Inn, with a very full Description of the Battle of Upton." "Chapter VI—From which it may be inferred, that the best Things are liable to be misunderstood and misinterpreted." There was no reason to read when she already knew what was going to happen next.

A man poked his head in the door. He was holding a chocolate and vanilla swirl ice-cream cone.

"Would you mind finishing that before you shop?" she asked politely. It was easy to be nice to the few customers who came in.

The bells jingled as he let the door slam behind him. He stood on the sidewalk staring at the window display. Winnie went back to her book. The next time she looked up he was gone, cone and all.

He was back the next day.

"No food this time," he announced and held up his hands. "I'm not even chewing gum." He opened his mouth and moved his tongue around his teeth as if she cared that he wasn't hiding anything. Winnie looked away.

"Can I help you with something in particular?" she asked. She began rearranging the bottle-cap belt buckles in the display case, though nothing was out of place. It was best to be doing something when customers came in. There was a tendency to become vulturelike in such a small shop. For the most part, she found her presence or assistance mattered very little in the customer's decision to buy or not.

"I've got something to ask you," he said.

His voice, which was strangely loud, as if his larynx were a loudspeaker, reminded her that she had forgotten to turn the cassette over. Suzanne only had a few tapes, all classical. She did not encourage Winnie to play the radio, though in the summer Winnie listened to the Pirates games in the late afternoons.

"Yes?" Winnie asked. Customers did not usually engage her in conversation.

"I want to know if you're interested in making some money," he asked. It was a warm afternoon, but the man was wearing a windbreaker. It was two-toned in team colors that Winnie did not recognize.

"That's what I'm doing," she said. She nodded to the leather coats chained to their steel racks, careful to include the men's motorcycle jackets on sale that she had arranged so that the cheapest items were the most accessible for customer inspection. If she was going to sell anything that month, it would probably be one of these pieces.

"How about a few extra bucks added to that paycheck this week?" The man had a salt-and-pepper goatee that needed trimming. "Does that interest you?"

Not really, Winnie thought. Though he carried no briefcase or portfolio, she guessed he was from Amway or one of the other pyramid companies. They had been by before. Winnie always enjoyed talking to people, but knew they were disappointed by her steadfast refusals.

"I bet I know what you want," the man said.

"Really?" Winnie asked.

"Sure," he nodded. "And I'm just the person to help you get it."

What Winnie wanted was an ocean. She would have liked to have beach property where at night or in the morning, depending on where the ocean was located, she could watch the sun setting or rising and feel the cool sand moving between her toes. She would like time to work on her tan. Of German and Irish descent, when Winnie spent time in the sun, she burned or freckled. But with the right creams, the right breezes, she was certain she could eventually change the color of her skin. She was fifty-three, too old to worry about skin cancer.

Money was not something she particularly wanted. "Are you building a casino?" she asked. Perhaps he wanted to talk to Suzanne. Suzanne and her husband were always talking money. She told him she was not interested. She undid the rubber band from her book and tried to remember where she had left the main characters.

He continued talking money to her, but she stayed with the

book, wishing he would go away. A few minutes later he left, promising that she'd see him again soon.

She was tired. Had it been her shop, she would have gone home, closed the curtains, turned the air-conditioning unit on high, and slept straight through the afternoon.

Winnie was slightly irritated when the man came in again the following afternoon. It was two o'clock, her normal break time, and she was anxious to leave the store.

"I'm back," he announced, all smiles.

"I can see that," she said. She flipped the OPEN sign around and stood jingling the keys. This was as rude as she could be.

He leaned into her. She took a step backward when suddenly he touched her face with his open palm. She slapped his hand away.

"Don't be afraid," he said.

Working in the shop bored her. Fear was not something she considered in her daily routine, though one time a guy with a gun had asked her to empty the cash register. She showed the would-be thief the credit card slips she collected in a pearl-laden jewelry box and tried to explain that they were not a cash kind of retail store. She invited him to take his choice of black leather jackets.

"I'm here to help you, not hurt you," he said.

"I don't want help," Winnie said.

"Are you afraid of something, little lady?" the man asked. "Is that why you won't talk to me?"

Winnie, especially opposed to people who called her lady, dear, or darling, did not know why she was talking to this man.

"Come on," he said. "Let me hear your fears."

"You want to know what I'm afraid of?" Winnie eyed the man suspiciously.

"Yes," he said. "Tell me your nightmares. What keeps you up at night?"

She thought for a minute.

"Rats," she told him. "I'm deathly afraid of rats." She had lived in New York for a short period of time when she was in her midtwenties, and she never forgot the sound of the rats scurrying in the wall beside her bed. She would have died if she had found one in her kitchen. She had seen the movie *Ben*, about a boy who befriended a rat, and while she liked the title song, the movie had given her nightmares.

"You're a funny lady," the man laughed.

I'm not, she wanted to tell him. I'm not funny at all. I'm a middle-aged, maybe even old woman who makes ten dollars an hour for doing nothing. I wash my hair three times a week and when I get drunk on red wine I stand in the dining room watching the shadow of my reflection in my plate glass window and pretend I'm Fantine from *Les Misérables*. Some nights I sob when I finish my solo number. One time I fell into the breakfront and broke the creamer from my wedding china. I'm twenty pounds overweight and the last man I had sex with was a police officer who gave me a parking ticket three days after we slept together. My son, who is too ashamed or too afraid to admit that he is gay, though I've known since he was twelve years old and won first place in the neighborhood Easy-Bake-Oven-Cook-Off, brings pretend girlfriends when he visits. They stay for one cocktail, then leave, as if he thinks I'm bedridden and boring. I take myself out to dinner when I need cheering up. You can't imagine how often a waitress can apologize for forgetting to put in your dinner order.

"Cynical maybe," she admitted to the stranger. "People have even called me bitter, and though I'd like to, I can't argue with that."

"You're not so bad-looking," he said. He whistled when she stood on her toes to check the clock over the Unitarian church two blocks west of Walnut Street.

"It's two o'clock," Winnie said. She was in the mood for a tuna melt on rye at Pamela's Country Kitchen. The waiter was a surly young man who hated working at the restaurant. He poured second and third cups of coffee without asking if she wanted refills. He never made small talk. He never asked her if everything was all right.

"I need a favor." The would-be thief unbuttoned his coat and fiddled with his tie. He did not exactly exude confidence, and Winnie could not imagine he was very successful in his ventures. His accent was Pittsburgh, but he was doing his best to hide this. He wore penny loafers with no socks, but the shoes were half a size too big, and the backs kept slipping off his foot. The leather made loud sucking noises every time he took a step.

"I don't think I can help you," Winnie said. He kept looking at her. His gaze was not flirtatious, but calculating. He was sizing her up for something. She wanted him to know that she was most definitely the wrong size.

"What have you got to lose if you listen to me?" he asked.

"Lunch," she said.

He shrugged as if her hunger was no big deal.

"I want you to listen to me," the man said. "That's it. Just listen to me."

"Listen to you?" Winnie asked.

"Yes, listen to me."

"If you're here to rob me, go ahead," Winnie said. "The store's insured big time. The stuff isn't mine. I won't put up a fight. You can tie me up, lock me in the dressing room, or let me roam the streets while you clear the place. There's no reason for shenanigans or tall tales if what you're really here for is to take the merchandise."

But it was his story he wanted her to hear.

"If you do nothing else for me," he begged, "at least listen to my story."

She was irritated and hungry, but nodded for him to go ahead—she would listen. He looked around for a seat, but there was only one and she was sitting in it. He would have to stand to tell his tale.

"I'm a cowboy," he told her. "A real old-fashioned round-'em-up outlaw." His accent became more southern.

"I'm a drifter, a rambler, a loner, a solitary man. I march to the beat of a different drum. You know I'm not someone who can be expected to play by society's rules. I'm just not like that."

"So?" Winnie interrupted. "What's the problem? Go be a cowboy."

"Even cowboys get the blues," he said.

Winnie put her hand on her hip and waited for him to continue. It took her a minute to understand that he had finished telling her what he wanted her to hear.

"My mother," he said when he saw her look of incomprehension.

Winnie was surprised. She had not been expecting a mother in his story.

His mother, it turned out, lived three blocks off Walnut Street. According to her son, she was sitting at home darning the socks of her long-dead husband. She was a rich woman who had promised her son his inheritance once he got married.

"So where's your wife?" Winnie asked.

"It's not easy to be married to a cowboy," the man said, and Winnie immediately understood the problem.

"Especially one who doesn't have any money," Winnie agreed.

"I'm bringing back my wife from Las Vegas to meet her. It turns out it's you."

"Me?" Winnie asked. Once again she was lost.

"If you want the job," the man said and held out his hand for her to shake. "There'll be something in it for you."

Winnie hesitated.

"I'm desperate. I wouldn't have come back to Pittsburgh if I wasn't desperate."

Winnie, well versed in desperation, agreed to help him. She would do it for half an hour only. She did not want to be paid.

He was not wearing a wedding ring, and Winnie asked if maybe they shouldn't stop at the toy store and buy fake diamonds or gold bands.

"The woman I marry," the man told her, "won't need rings or jewelry to know that I love her."

"She might not need it, but she might like it," Winnie said.

The woman lived in a brick house surrounded by red and pink geraniums. Her living room was filled with cuttings from her flower beds. The pink of the geraniums matched the pink trim of the throw pillows. Winnie accepted a cup of tea.

Winnie, who was supposed to be from Vegas, had changed into a pair of leather pants. Size twelve—they were tight across her behind. The smell of new leather was fierce and she did what she could to ignore it. She had accessorized with a bolo tie with a sterling-silver lizard at the neck that kept bobbing up and hitting her under the chin.

The woman smiled at Winnie, then poured herself a glass of single malt scotch whiskey. She swirled the amber liquid around the three ice cubes, then lifted her glass into the air. "Bottoms up," she said determinedly. Winnie recognized this woman. She was obviously someone who was used to toasting and drinking to herself.

Winnie had half a mind to join her. She finished the tepid tea in two swallows and held out her cup for the mother to fill.

The son kneaded Winnie in the ribs and whispered for her to act like a wife from Las Vegas. Winnie forced her thoughts toward cactus and slot machines. She tried to look as empty as the desert air.

But hell, Las Vegas. They drank like fish in Las Vegas.

And she was from Vegas. She should drink.

"Might as well do me too with that magic," Winnie said.

Winnie praised the woody taste of the scotch.

"To good health," the mother said.

"And long lives," Winnie agreed.

Winnie asked to see photographs of the man when he was a young boy. The mother smiled as if praising Winnie's effort. She made no move to bring out her photo albums.

Winnie would have liked the opportunity to tell the mother about her own son. He lived three miles away, yet never called. She knew almost nothing about what he did in his life. His weekly visits were painful, the bother evident in his strained conversations. He often turned on the television and pretended to be interested in the local news, though she knew he hated everything about living in Pittsburgh.

Winnie had been at the Arts and Crafts Show in Mellon Park last spring when she saw her son browsing the ceramic bowls in the tent booths. When he turned and saw Winnie, he and his young friend took off running. Winnie, thinking there was something wrong, followed him down the stone steps. Then she realized why he was running away from her.

Winnie covered her mouth, but not before a small burp escaped.

The mother had a list of things she wanted done around the house. The son agreed to fix the VCR so the green light would not flash 12:00 all day long, but after much fidgeting he admitted defeat. He was too tired to look at the garbage disposal. He had no idea why the back door scraped the cement step when she tried to close it.

He flipped through the Yellow Pages and tore out a section. "Call this number," he told his mother. "A handyman will come and do whatever you need done. I know you can afford someone to help you around the place."

The mother sighed. The skin around her mouth tightened. Winnie recognized the way the woman held her tongue. She did not have the freedom to criticize. This was not right.

The mother did not want a stranger fixing her things. She wanted her son to be there. The house and its repairs were just an excuse.

Another round of cocktails, another plate of sausage and cheese hors d'oeuvres, and the conversation lagged.

The mother and Winnie discussed the shrinking parking situation in the neighborhood.

"At least I've got a garage," the mother said.

"Isn't that the truth?" Winnie agreed.

There was no need to pretend anymore. Winnie understood this. The mother had read the situation correctly. She had recognized Winnie for who she was—an impostor. And though disappointed in the way the afternoon had turned out, she could not be angry. Like the tables of contents in the novels Winnie read, the mother knew what was going to happen long before it happened. The living chapter titles told the whole story. The mother stared into her glass. Loneliness like that could make you crazy. There was nothing you could buy or sell to stop it from taking over your life. When her son left she would be alone.

Whether or not she gave him the money, she would be alone. It was that simple.

The man stood up and kissed his mother on the cheek, promising to see her in the morning. Winnie shook the mother's hand. "It's been a pleasure meeting you." Had she had a card with her name and number, she would have left it on the coffee table. Had she been alone, she would have stayed for another glass of scotch. She would have done what she could to write a surprise twist into Chapter XV—In Which Mrs. Martin and a Lonely Widow Drink a Whole Bottle of Scotch, or maybe a new chapter, In Which a Very Funny Fifty-Year-Old Explains How to Have Fun with a Bit of Overdyed Leather Even When You Have a Large Rear End.

Once on the street, the man walked as if in pain. Winnie asked if he was going to be sick. "It's my bladder," he complained.

"Doesn't your mother have indoor plumbing?"

"I couldn't leave you two alone."

Winnie agreed that that would have been dangerous. There was no telling the kind of trouble two lonely women could get into, especially when they had jackass liars for sons.

"You were supposed to be my wife," he said. "A woman my mother could respect. Instead you drank scotch, snorted at her jokes, and ate the whole plate of hors d'oeuvres."

"I skipped lunch because of you," Winnie said.

"No one is that hungry," he said.

"You should have brought the woman you vowed to love eternally," Winnie said.

"I don't have a woman," he said.

"Then don't take your mother's money," Winnie said.

"You don't understand," he said.

"Listen," she commanded so loudly he had no choice but to

do what she said. "The open road is calling. And it's not for me. You better hop to it."

The man did not look like he was wanting to ramble anywhere that night.

"You want my advice?" she asked.

"Not at all."

"Go back home. Talk to your mother. Tell her the truth. Explain your situation. Don't leave anything out."

The son looked at her once then walked away, scurrying as if he was afraid she would follow. Winnie stood her ground, not quite finished with the advice she had to give.

"This summer the two of you should go to Three Rivers Stadium. Stand in line and buy season tickets to the Pirates. There's been a baseball strike. People are suspicious of the stability of the ball clubs—you'll be able to get bleacher seats. When the vendor comes around and says what'll it be, she might want a few jumbo beers. I say let her have 'em."

He was at the end of the block. In a minute he would disappear from her sight. "Did you hear me?" Winnie shouted. "Jumbo beers. Hot dogs with onions and relish. Soft pretzels soaked in mustard. She's a hungry woman. Let her go for it."

The coffee drinkers sitting at the outside cafe were staring at her. She turned away, lest they mistake her for a ranting, raving bag lady.

She walked quickly to the Uni-Mart on Ellsworth Avenue. The sign on the door told her that this franchise strictly enforced the "Only TWO children at ONE time rule." She shopped the three aisles quickly. She picked up some frozen microwavable burritos that were decent if you used a good sauce and a bit of canned black beans. To drink, she chose a bottle of raspberry-flavored sparkling water.

When she handed him a twenty-dollar bill, the cashier asked her if she had anything smaller.

"Just some change," she said and shook her wallet so he could hear the jingle of pennies and nickels.

He shrugged and held out his hands as if to say that there was nothing he could do to help her.

To go home without her purchases would have been pathetic. She wrote her name on the receipt and handed it to the cashier, whose blue uniform jacket was unzipped to reveal a wrinkled white button-down.

"Here you go," she said, her voice sounding bossy. "I'll come in tomorrow with something smaller. I live around the corner."

"I don't think my boss will go for that."

"Don't worry. You'll get your money," Winnie said. "You can count on me."

"I'm not sure," the guy hesitated. Winnie scooped up her purchases and walked out of the store with a big friendly wave.

That was it. She had nothing more to say to anybody. Her day was done.

Three Fat Women of (Pittsburgh Just Visiting) Antibes

NE WAS CALLED JANE AND WAS a divorcée. The second was born Margaret Mary but had her name legally changed to Amber when she turned twenty-one. Sally was the third. She had never been married, never been engaged, never even had what others would consider a longtime serious boyfriend. A virgin, yes, though she no longer admitted or complained about it.

The women were in their late thirties and comfortably overweight, so when they talked about food (and who doesn't when traveling, especially when traveling in France?) they spoke not in terms of enjoyment but in terms of negotiations, as if everything they ate or drank had a price.

"We must have walked five miles," Jane said.

"At least," Sally sighed, as if they had just finished exercising.

"If you count what we did on the boardwalk, add that to the museum tour, I figure it's more like six," Amber said. She recorded her daily activities in a compact datebook she carried in her purse. Most nights she exaggerated her exercise and lied about her caloric intake.

"Maybe more," Jane said.

"But at least five," Amber said and snapped the rubber band around her little black book.

The three were good friends. They understood each other's foibles, tolerated each other's moods. They were kind to each other. Usually.

This was their fourth trip abroad, and they traveled well together. They were intelligent enough to understand that women were complicated, sensitive creatures, who sometimes had to be dramatically unreasonable. Almost a week into the trip, and no one had cried or thrown a hissy fit. There had been moments—the tiff at the Picasso museum had been particularly tense—but even that had passed after early evening cocktails.

The women were at their best when it came to food. Breakfast, lunch, and dinner were things they never argued about. Unlike some tourists who opted to share meals, the trio from Pittsburgh always ordered full dinners. They were not shy about a third bottle of wine. Dessert was included in the price of the meal and would have been wasteful to refuse. After-dinner brandies, certainly a special treat, were never considered an indulgence.

Night six of their two-week excursion, and they decided to treat themselves to dinner at Les Vieux Murs, an expensive seafood restaurant near the castle in Antibes.

The waiter, who later identified himself as the owner of the place, greeted them in English, tripping over verb tenses until

Jane urged him to speak French. The women were well educated. All three were fluent in French, and each spoke a smatter-
ing of another language. It was one reason they enjoyed traveling
together—things were so much easier to obtain when you had
the vocabulary.

"The chef has not yet arrived, but rest assured, he will be here
momentarily," he told the women. "When he comes I will tell
him to cook his best for three women who look like angels."

He presented them with a tray of pretty pink aperitifs—
complimentary Kir Royales in champagne flutes. They forgave
him for his tardy welcome, but when he walked away from the
table, Sally wrinkled her nose. "My god. What a cheeseball," she
said.

"I don't know," Jane said and sniffled. "I think he's kind of
cute."

"You think everyone's cute," Amber scolded. "But you never
do anything about it." She would have liked to talk to Jane about
her lack of love-life, but men was a subject they had given up
discussing because it was the same record playing over and over
again.

"No. Oh no," Jane said, blushing and stammering like a little
girl. "I don't. I never would."

Amber knew that Jane had been married. But the ex-husband
was persona non grata except in the vaguest of terms. He entered
conversations as a whispery shadow of the past, mostly as a warning to stay away. Sally, on the other hand, had never slept with a
man, and, even when inebriated, was coy about the future of her
virginity. They thought Amber was loose—too eager to meet
men. They were not afraid to criticize her for at least trying to
change her life. A spinster was not something one aspired to be.
Amber wished they admired her more for her courage to go after

what she wanted. She had bad luck with men, but she was always the first to admit it.

The three women had met at an Attr-ACTIVE Women's Group at the Jewish Community Center in the Pittsburgh neighborhood of Squirrel Hill. The brochure described the once-a-week meetings as a unique opportunity for women who wanted change in their lives. "Here is a physical fitness approach to emotional and spiritual well-being." The meetings would consist of discussions about diet, exercise, and an attitude adjustment, which would—hopefully—result in a more attractive woman.

The group leader was a large, talkative woman named Rosemary, who established in the first few minutes of the initial meeting that she was not a leader, but an encourager. "Attr-ACTIVE women do not want or need leaders. We are not lemmings. We are our own growing and developing women—we are ourselves." She stood, then bent over and moved her hands up and down her feet. It was a remarkable physical feat for such a heavyset woman. A few members stood and tried to touch their toes. Amber stayed in her seat. As Rosemary had encouraged, she was not going to follow.

Rosemary was in favor of strong declarative statements. They had punch but not much meaning. She used these key phrases in her own speech and tried to get the group to adopt them.

"Turn the beat around," she advised when a group member complained that she could not find time in her hectic life for a workout. "Accentuate the positive."

"Get a pet," Rosemary suggested. "A dog is an exercise machine with hair and a warm tongue," she claimed. "I used to come home after a stressful day at work and go straight for junk food and television. Now I come home and take my dog for a

39

long walk. I've made new friends. I've gotten to know my neighborhood. I've turned the beat around and couldn't be happier."

Amber had joined the group to meet educated women in similar socioeconomic situations, not to listen to the obvious pathologies of those in need of professional guidance. She got enough of that from the "Dr. Laura" radio show every afternoon. Amber did not know what her "unique stuff inside," another of Rosemary's phrases, was, and she did not understand how canoeing would help her find it. Still, she had paid her seventy-nine dollars and thought it best not to quit midstream.

"If you can organize your kitchen, you can organize your life." Rosemary announced one night. A canceled pet-sitter had forced her to bring the new puppy to the meeting. He sat at her heels, slowly chewing the hem out of her skirt.

Jane snorted. "Oh come on. Get real."

Sally giggled, though whether she was amused by Jane's retort or by the puppy was not clear.

Amber, who had been napping with her eyes open, woke to the sound of irritation and ridicule.

"No fighting," Rosemary said and began touching her toes frantically.

"All I said was I wasn't sure I followed the logic of that statement," Jane said. "Surely you agree that someone can have a perfectly neat house and a cluttered life."

Rosemary stopped exercising and began to whimper. "Anger is so tiring. It just wears me down." She grabbed the Kleenex box and buried her face.

Jane stood. "I'm not angry. I simply asked a question. You're not afraid of discussion, are you?"

"I'm not having a good week," Rosemary sobbed. "I used to come home after a stressful day at work, have a junk-food bonanza complete with reruns on "Nick at Nite." Now I come home to find that my stupid dog has chewed my new ninety dollar black pumps into bite-sized pieces. The minute I walk in the door he starts barking, begging for a walk. Even when it's zero degrees outside. I can't cope. He's making my life a miserable mess, and I don't know what to do."

"Why don't you get rid of him?" Sally asked.

"This is ridiculous," Jane judged, walking out of the room.

The other Attr-ACTIVE women scurried to form a protective ring around their leader. "There, there, dear," they comforted. "There. There."

The Squirrel Cage, which was less than a block from the JCC, served a Cheeseburger Platter that included french fries with a choice of gravy or homemade ranch dressing for $3.95. Amber, Jane, and Sally ordered full platters and a pitcher of draft beer, not caring that the hand-washed mugs tasted of dishwashing soap. There they decided a trip abroad would do more to enhance their lives than a two-hour meeting in a chlorine-smelling, windowless room of the local JCC.

"Don't go to the hardware store for milk," Amber quoted their leader. Rosemary's adages worked best when taken out of context.

"The best thing about a cocktail party is being asked to it," Jane remembered.

"Gluttony is not a secret vice," Sally said.

Her new friends agreed.

The owner/waiter at the restaurant in Antibes served them a second round of Kir Royales, then scurried away from the table before they could ask him for anything else.

"Maybe he could bring us a photograph of some food," Sally

said sardonically. She had taken her scarf and tied it around her head. The style might have been reminiscent of Grace Kelly in *To Catch a Thief*, but Sally looked more like an old woman suffering from a bad toothache.

"Should we go somewhere else?" Amber said.

"Leave? After two free drinks?" Jane said. "That would be rude." Jane returned to her menu. Amber wouldn't be surprised if her friend had it memorized.

Amber raised her glass of Kir and held it at eye level. "Look," she told her friends. "I'm looking at the world through rose-colored glasses." Jane and Sally were deep in discussion about the next day's plan. If they heard her, they were ignoring her.

Amber was slightly disappointed by the trip to the Riviera. They had chosen Antibes because it was supposed to be the spot where the really really rich and the very very successful still lived. But Amber had not seen anyone who did not look like a tourist. Everyone walked around in comfortable tennis shoes or dull-colored Rockports, their compact passport carriers slung over their shoulder. Mostly Americans, none of them exotic or interesting.

The general feeling of the area was not successful or rich, but gray—like rain on a Sunday afternoon.

Amber lowered her glass and the soft-colored world disappeared.

"I'm going out for cigarettes," she said, and dumped her purse onto the table and began separating the francs from the U.S. coins.

"You begged us never to let you smoke again," Jane reminded her.

"I'll buy the pack but just smoke one," Amber said, holding up her two fingers in the Girl Scout promise. Cigarettes were not potato chips. It was possible to be satisfied with one or two.

"Fat chance," Sally snorted. She tucked her chin back into her scarf.

"It's not my fault they don't sell them individually," Amber said, wondering why Sally had chosen the word fat.

"Do what you want, but don't bitch to us tomorrow when you wake up with a nicotine hangover from your largesse." Jane said.

"Right. Right. Right," Amber said, now convinced that Sally's word selection was below the belt. She scooped up a handful of coins and left the damp restaurant.

The tobacco shop was closed, its front door locked. A man stood beside the cash register counting money and smoking a cigarette. Amber knocked.

"Fermé," he mouthed and pointed to the sign hanging in the doorway.

She put her hands together as if praying.

He smiled. His teeth were white and beautifully straight. He unlocked the door and let her in.

"Hello, pretty woman," he said.

Amber finally found what she had been looking for. Jackpot. Right here in Antibes.

He would not give change, so she bought four packs of American cigarettes. He did not charge her for matches but asked if she would like a tour of the city.

"The beach is particularly beautiful at night," he said.

Europe was magical. This would never have happened to her in Pittsburgh.

Amber could see the expressions of curiosity when she and Maurice walked into the restaurant.

"Meet my new friend," she said grandly. The table was covered with cracker crumbs. Sally and Jane looked tired and tipsy.

Maurice moved around the table giving both Jane and Sally kisses on the cheeks. So polite and so French, utterly romantic, thought Amber, pleased with her find. She was thrilled, almost giddy.

"You must be sisters," Maurice said. His French was lovely, all *r*'s and throat sounds. Amber wanted to kiss his language.

"You look so much alike," Maurice said.

"Imagine that," Sally giggled. She laughed so hard she spat up the bubbles of her champagne. "The three of us, sisters?"

Amber did not look like her friends. They did dress alike— all of them wore a sort of traveling uniform. Identical black stretch pants, one hundred percent cotton with expandable elastic waistbands, perfect for hand washing in hotel bidets. On top they wore shapeless shirts, long sweaters, oversized vests. They dressed like onions, shedding layers as the afternoon sun rose in the Mediterranean sky, adding them when the chill of evening moved in. It was mere coincidence that Amber and Sally were wearing the same color Limited Express pullover that night. But Sally looked like someone's Russian grandmother, and Jane, with the pen sticking out of the bun at the back of her head, looked anything but pretty.

"Maurice and I are going for a walk," Amber announced, deliberately changing the subject.

"What about dinner?" Jane asked.

"What about it?" Amber asked. Food was the least of her desires.

"Should we order for you?" Jane said, taking the pen from her bun as if she meant to write down Amber's dinner request.

"Do what you like," Amber said and looked into Maurice's dark, dark eyes. His lashes were graying on the tips, giving him a gentle look. "And I'll do the same."

"Be careful," Sally warned.

"Oh, I don't think we'll have sex on the beach," Amber said, knowing full well that Sally had not been talking about sex.

When Amber returned a short time later, she was alone.

She opened her menu, not wanting to answer any of their nosy questions about Maurice. "What'd you order for me?" she asked Jane, not caring that she had interrupted their conversation.

Jane pointed to the third item on the menu.

"You ordered me liver?" Amber asked.

Jane nodded. "You had fish last night, I figured you'd enjoy a nice piece of meat tonight."

"Liver is not a nice piece of meat," Amber said. "It is a waste-filtering organ." She reached for the breadbasket, but it was empty. Suddenly famished, she sneered at Jane.

Jane slapped her hand away. "Someone had better be careful."

"Where's your new friend?" Sally said, obviously trying to change the subject. "What was his name? Mario? Morris?"

"Maurice is running an errand. It's a matter of business and shouldn't take more than a few moments. He's coming to get me in a few minutes," Amber said. She realized how thin his excuse sounded. But it was the truth. He had promised her he'd be right back for her.

Sally laughed aloud.

"You don't know him," Amber said, coming to Maurice's defense a bit forcefully, considering her doubts. "He said he'd be back and I believe him."

"You don't really know him either," Sally said.

"Just because I have someone new in my life doesn't mean you have to get jealous," Amber said smugly. "Green is not a color women wear well."

Sally rolled her eyes. "Someone new?" She looked under the

table as if searching for something. "Someone new. However short-lived."

Amber was hungry for a fight. "Well, it's not like you've got any men in your life."

"Remind me again how many men you've had over the years?" Sally asked. "Fifty? Sixty? Or is three hundred a better guess?"

"At least I've had some," Amber said.

"Like the ex-con?" Sally hissed.

"I went out with him. I never said I slept with him," Amber said. But she had.

"The pizza delivery guy, Julia's uncle, your ex-boss." Sally listed men Amber would have rather forgotten. "All fine examples of your better taste in men."

"I'm warning you," Amber held up her fist and shook it at Sally.

"Oh, skip the threats," Sally said.

"Take this as notice, then," Amber said, and turned her hand in front of her mouth as if closing a lock. She was never going to speak to Sally again.

"You really are too big for your britches," Sally said.

"I'm too big," Amber said. Again with the wordplay.

"I didn't mean it literally," Sally said.

"Perhaps she just meant it figure-atively." Jane leaned across the table.

"I wasn't talking about weight," Sally said, her face pink with embarrassment.

"I guess not," Amber said. "You never do." She puffed out her cheeks like a blowfish.

The noises they made at each other were like cats hissing.

Amber looked over just as Maurice walked into the restaurant. She had not really expected to see him again, and she stood, knocking her champagne glass to the floor. It shattered when it hit the stone tiles.

"Maurice," she cried dramatically and kissed him on the lips. She left the table without saying a word to her friends.

Maurice and Amber walked arm in arm through the streets of Antibes.

He was nice. Curious to know about her life back in Pittsburgh, he asked a zillion questions. Amber liked the attention. The night air was pink, the setting sun glowed with her happiness. When they got to the beach, they began kissing frantically. The pine taste of his cologne coated her tongue, reminding her that she had not eaten since noon.

She could feel the sand in her sandals. Her sunburned skin felt fresh and alive. She was not being stupid. Not with Maurice. She wasn't dreaming. She wasn't counting on wedding bells, as Sally always insisted she did. It felt nice to be appreciated. This is what life was all about. It was a shame she didn't meet men like this more often.

Maurice led her to the center of town, where, at the condom machine, he asked her for some money. She gave him one of her one hundred franc notes, which he slid into the opening before turning the knob. Her change spilled onto the street like money rolling from a slot machine. She was giddy and told him not to bother with the few francs that had rolled into the gutter.

"Don't be silly," he scolded and pocketed all that he collected.

The hotel across from the train station was dingy. The smell of cooked and cooking cabbage was everywhere. The bedspread was worn, the rug was mustard-colored and stained, and the window had no view except of the tracks, which might have been construed as romantic if the sun had been shining.

"It's certainly not the Ritz," she said.

The lamp beside the bed did not work. Had she been with Sally and Jane, they would have taken one look and walked out. They did not suffer dingy surroundings. A clean and well-equipped bathroom was essential to a pleasant stay. But Amber did not want to give the impression of being an American snob, so she squinted her eyes until the room took on a nice glow and told Maurice she was having a good time.

Maurice put his arms around her waist. "I have never loved so big," he said. It sounded romantic in French and she was not at all embarrassed to undress in front of him.

He kissed her lips. "Your lips are so pretty," he cooed, and she believed him.

He kissed her eyes. "Your eyes are so pretty."

Her throat. "Your throat is so pretty."

Her ears. "Your ears are so pretty."

Her hair. "Your hair. . . ."

Amber felt as if she were in the middle of a bad French lesson, but she did not want it to stop.

When they finished making love, Maurice asked for money.

"A few hundred francs, my pretty one," he said in the same low throaty voice he had used to woo her.

Amber sat up in bed, fully awake, absolutely ravenous. She was sure a hotel directly across from the train station did not have room service.

"I need money." Maurice shook her leg when he saw that she was not listening to his request. "I was supposed to meet a man tonight. That was my job. Instead I spent the time with you. Now I need the money."

"I suppose you do," Amber said. The disappointment of the night spread through her body like a sharp pain. She bit her lip, not daring to cry.

She would not let him ruin her night. She leaned over and kissed Maurice's hands. "Your hands," she said in English, "are so pretty."

Maurice, no longer interested in giving or receiving language lessons, rolled off the bed and got dressed.

"Sex, if you ask me, is highly overrated," Amber said. "All that talk about how many calories it uses," she said. "But really all you do is lie there on your back. Doesn't seem to burn anything."

"You're very big," Maurice said without emotion. "You must have lots of money." It no longer sounded romantic.

"You probably burn more calories trying to find the channel switcher during a good night of television watching. All in all it's a real waste of time," Amber declared.

Amber was upset, but not surprised. Her track record with men was annoyingly consistent. Sally had been right. She asked Maurice to walk her back to the hotel and he grunted something about a restaurant. She followed, thinking food, wine, or both might salvage something of the evening.

Instead Maurice took her to a crowded nightclub. He walked in ahead of her, and she lost him in the crowd.

In the small bathroom, a woman stood over the sink, gagging herself with her two fingers. Amber did not need to hear her speak to know she was American.

"You shouldn't do that," Amber said. "It will make you sick."

"That's the point," the woman said.

American magazines and television were filled with horror stories about women like these, but Amber had never seen one in action. She watched the young woman throw up with abject fascination. Amber put her hands on her own hips, feeling the thickness, the bulk of her extra weight. And for the first time in years, she felt the strange pull of doubt, feelings she hadn't had since she was fifteen. She brought her finger to her mouth and pushed it past her lips, down her throat, until she could feel herself gagging.

She saw herself in the mirror and her mind cleared instantly. However disappointing the night had been, she would not turn stupid. She would not be ridiculous.

"Stop," Amber said. She pulled on the woman's dress. "Stop this nonsense."

"Have you ever been thin?" the woman removed her fingers from her throat and talked to Amber in the mirror.

Amber considered the question. "Not exactly."

"Then go away," she said. Her nose was runny. She reached for a piece of paper toweling, then dropped it to the ground when she had finished with it.

"Very glamorous," Amber said. "Unbelievably romantic."

"I locked the door," the young woman said. "I didn't mean to be a public spectacle. I didn't expect a group discussion." She grabbed her hair in a ponytail and bent over the sink again.

Amber knew she was talking to a woman who would never sign up for an Attr-ACTIVE Women's Group at the Jewish Community Center. But she was probably worth saving.

"The discovery of a new dish does more for human happiness than the discovery of a new star," Amber said. This was not one of Rosemary's, but considering the situation, it was appropriate—and probably true.

The thin woman rolled her eyes. "Leave me alone, you weirdo." Amber had no idea why skinny women were so stupid.

"Food is a pleasure. One should eat breakfast like a king, lunch like a prince, and dinner like a queen."

"I would never eat a meal," the woman said. "Ever." She turned to the side and admired her thin shape in the cracked mirror.

Amber realized that she was wasting her words on this creature, but she felt empowered, full of strength and wisdom. She put all thoughts of the Maurice disaster aside and talked with pride and conviction. "The kitchen is a country in which there are always discoveries to be made. Eating is the one passionate thing left to us in these bleak times."

"I don't want to discover anything," the woman said. "I just want to be skinny. That's what I want." She extracted a small tube of toothpaste from her purse. She squeezed a thin line onto her finger and moved it around her mouth, all odor disguised by the mint flavoring. "What I don't want," she said, brushing her hair back with her fingertips, "is to end up like you."

"You'll never be like me," Amber said. "Never." Not one to exert herself in a useless cause, Amber stopped talking.

The hotel room, with its smells of lavender soap, cinnamon candles, and peanut butter–chocolate treats, was at once warm and welcoming. Jane and Sally were asleep. Their thick noisy shapes, cocooned in extra blankets and pillows, made her weep with relief. She got under the covers and waited for morning.

Jane and Sally were her friends. She should not have fought with them. It was up to her to apologize—an act she would have to do with a great deal of care. She would have to be humble.

At first light she went downstairs to reserve their favorite table on the seaside terrace, then waited for them to come to breakfast.

Sally and Jane walked outside a short while later. They had showered and looked fresh and ready for a full day of sightseeing.

"How was dinner?" Amber asked, waving them over to the table.

"Excellent," Sally said.

"Your liver was delicious," Jane said. "You owe me 150 francs. There are no refunds in four-star French restaurants."

Amber pulled out the money and handed it across the table. It was going to be rough. They would not let her off easily.

Jane read the newspaper. Sally flipped through the travel guide. They were doing a good job of ignoring her.

She was not sure they were listening, but she went ahead with her plan.

"I was thinking," Amber said slowly. "The Hôtel Negresco in Nice has a very good lunch deal. Four-course gourmet meal for two hundred francs, which is actually quite reasonable," she paused and then added, "as long as you don't convert it into dollars."

She bribed them slowly and carefully. "It's probably my turn to treat you both to a good meal."

Jane looked up from the *International Herald Tribune*. "Duck is very good this time of year. Even here on the Riviera. I wonder if the Negresco has duck."

"It says here that the dining room has a domed ceiling decorated with twenty-four-carat gold leaf and the biggest carpet ever to come out of the Savonnerie workshops," Sally read from Jane's pocket guide to the Riviera. "The chandelier was commissioned from Baccarat by Czar Nicholas II. It doesn't sound like the kind of place that wouldn't have duck."

Amber nodded. "Yes. We could have duck."

"Although duck is very fatty," Sally sniffed.

"The walk from the train station to the Matisse museum is two miles," Jane said, jotting some numbers on her newspaper.

"We could do a quick tour of Antibes," Sally said. "I still have to go to the post office. Twice around the old town could be part of our constitutional today."

"That's good," Jane said. "That'll put us way ahead. We should be all ready for a nice big lunch."

They turned to Amber and nodded their approval.

"I'll make a reservation after breakfast," Amber promised.

"Whoever said money could not buy happiness does not know where to shop," Sally clapped her hands—an Attr-ACTIVE woman, even here on the Côte d'Azur.

"The only dangerous food is wedding cake," Jane said. They had heard this one before.

A slight breeze passed over the table, and with it came a moment of silence. Amber looked at her friends and thought that only a Frenchman would say they looked like angels. They should stay in Antibes forever.

The waiter arrived with their breakfast tray. And though the French have taken to buying their pastries and baguettes frozen and in bulk, the croissants at the women's hotel were served fresh and warm. There was always plenty of butter. Plenty of jam. Plenty of preserves. Honey or clotted cream upon request.

This Month of Charity

AROL'S STUDENT HAS FEW PROBLEMS with individual words—it is sentences that give him trouble. Donald, her fifty-four-year-old student, begins the new paragraph, reading just above a whisper, then stops before the end of the second line. The Detroit Public Library is busy with people checking out books, and Carol concentrates on the shuffling noise at the circulation desk rather than on the silence in front of her. Donald lowers his head and moves his finger across the page.

"There are fifteen words in this sentence. It's too long." He shows Carol the book as if she won't believe his claim.

"You know the words," Carol says again. This is their first night working together, and she tries to be patient, but Donald has been complaining about sentence length since they started. "Read it aloud. Slowly. Then you'll understand what it means."

"Adults read to themselves," Donald protests. "I don't want to read like a beginner."

Carol knows that in ancient times only the most intelligent people could read without voicing the words. Julius Caesar was considered to be a genius because he read without moving his lips. Messengers would stare in awe as he read the news of the State—his mind understanding, his body not showing any struggle.

Carol keeps her thoughts to herself. She does not like teaching people to read and knows her lack of enthusiasm makes her a less-than-average teacher. She only volunteered for the program because she is attracted to her next-door neighbor, Mitch, who is also doing volunteer work. She thought these nights of charity would bring them closer together. So far this has not happened.

Donald asks if they can take a water break and Carol agrees. When they return to their table, Donald finishes the article and they discuss his understanding of the material. At nine o'clock they carry the books back to the special program desk. Carol takes out his file and records what they've read and how much progress she feels he's made. His former reading teacher has made several notes, and Carol learns that Donald is serious about learning but easily distracted. He is also unusually talkative about his personal life.

Once outside, Donald offers her a ride. It is late June and the sky is full of pastel pinks and blues. The sun, like the kids playing tag in the parking lot, is stalling nightfall.

"My friend's here." Carol points to the car parked in front of the library, where Mitch is waiting with his emergency lights flashing. Mitch has told her that he admires the way she cares about her students, and she wants him to see her talking with Donald.

"I look forward to seeing you again." She dawdles for a moment to impress Mitch.

"Thank you for your help," Donald says. "You're a very good teacher."

Carol blushes. No one has ever praised her for her work. She's not certain she deserves it, but she's pleased by the compliment.

"Is that a new one?" Mitch asks when she gets into the car. The air conditioner is on high, and Carol shivers with goosebumps.

"New to me, but not a beginner," Carol says. "His other teacher just quit the program, so I got him." Her body adjusts to the cool air, and the bumps on her arm disappear. She asks Mitch how his night went.

"Dull. We went back to the house and watched videos."

"Did he talk?"

"Three, maybe four words," Mitch says. "I feel like quitting. If this is what it means to be a Big Brother, I don't want to do it. I'm not helping him like this."

Mitch's little brother is fourteen years old and quiet. He prefers to watch cable TV at Mitch's house rather than play baseball or visit Boblo Island, an amusement park on the Detroit River—things Mitch had planned to do with him. One night he asked Mitch if he could mow his lawn, and Mitch told him he could do it whenever he wanted. It's the only thing he shows any interest in.

"You can't quit. We're in this together," Carol says. If Mitch quits doing volunteer work, they won't have a reason to see each other.

Mitch nods and asks if Carol wants to eat pizza. She agrees, though she doesn't like the Italian restaurant in their neighborhood. The place is too loud, too bright, and there are always too many people. She and Mitch are not lovers, but Carol has been attracted to him ever since he bought the house next door. He is exactly the kind of person she wants to date. He is kind. He is interesting. He is good-looking. He has a job. He has all his hair and he doesn't complain about every little thing—a trait she finds difficult to deal with in both men and women, but especially annoying in men. Carol is used to men's attention, and Mitch's aloofness confuses as well as depresses her. As it stands, she has no idea whether he finds her sexually interesting, even mildly attractive.

On Thursday the secretary from the Literacy Program calls Carol at work and relays the message that Donald will not be able to make tonight's lesson. He wants to reassure Carol that he's serious about learning and that he will definitely be there next week. Carols takes the black magic marker and draws a large *X* on her desk calendar. Then she calls Mitch and pretends to be relieved that she has a week's reprieve from the volunteer job. She tells him that she'd still like to get together for dinner. Mitch asks if he and his little brother can watch TV at her house. The temperature at noon was in the upper nineties, and he knows his house will be a hotbox.

"My living room's not air-conditioned," Carol says. "We could sit out on the back porch. There might be some sort of breeze."

"Let's move the TV into the air conditioning," Mitch says. "I have to get out of this heat."

"That's fine." Carol is delighted with Mitch's suggestion and considers it progress that he knows that her bedroom is air-conditioned. She thinks again how uncomplicated it would be to start an intimate relationship with Mitch. They are already friends. They are familiar with each other's tastes in restaurants, movies, and other kinds of entertainment. They own almost identical homes. There would be none of the awkward getting to know one another that Carol finds so boring.

At six-thirty Mitch and Kevin arrive carrying stacks of styrofoam cartons full of take-out ribs. The milk shakes are dripping through the paper bag. They stain Mitch's clean T-shirt with circles of chocolate. Carol opens everything in the sink and transfers it to paper plates. She has been too hot to think about eating, and she doesn't know how they'll finish the heavy slabs of ribs, the quarts of coleslaw.

Mitch spreads a plastic tablecloth on the floor in front of the TV stand and the three of them eat picnic-style watching the news. Mitch is wearing shorts, and the hair on his legs is wet with perspiration. Carol watches him while he eats. Kevin is quiet, but seems pleased with the meal. He is engrossed in the television and seems to get more of the jokes than Carol does.

The food makes Carol listless. The night is duller than she had imagined. She tries to stay awake but nods off during one of the situation comedies. She jerks up when she hears Kevin's laugh. Mitch is in the kitchen trying to stuff all the paper trash into the small trash can. She opens a garbage bag for him and he fills it.

"It'd be easier to adopt a child overseas," Mitch jokes. "Think how simple it would be to mail in seventy-two cents a day."

"That's not the point." It occurs to her that maybe the only reason he is sticking out the volunteer job is that he wants to see her. This thought pleases her.

He smiles. "Watching three hours of TV a night is?" He pushes the hair off her face and tucks it behind her ear. He is always doing things like this—touching her in small ways that make Carol feel he'd be a caring lover. They are alone. It is just the moment that he should kiss her. She waits, but he goes to the sink and washes the barbecue sauce off his hands.

As soon as Kevin and Mitch leave, Carol goes to bed. She thinks of Mitch's hand on her face and knows that they are getting closer. The next morning she's awake by five-thirty, feeling refreshed and ready for the day to begin. She showers, dresses for work, and then sits on the front porch with her coffee and last night's newspaper. The air is gray, and waking noises strike like echoes as they move across the silent city.

Mitch's side door slams shut, and Carol watches a woman walk down the drive. The woman smiles and says good morning, but Carol is too surprised to react. Instead she looks down at the newspaper in her lap and tries to understand the bold print of the headlines. Carol hears the sound of an engine, then the hum of tires, as a red Toyota disappears around the corner.

She knows it's not fair. It's not fair that Mitch slept with a woman after spending the evening with her. He has never mentioned that he was seeing anyone, and Carol suspects he kept it from her deliberately. She feels betrayed by his touch in the kitchen—betrayed that he would go on to touch someone else more intimately.

Though it is only six-fifteen, Carol decides to leave for the hospital where she works. She doesn't care how early she arrives. Her coffee cup is half full when she throws it at Mitch's bedroom window. She wants him to know that she's seen his woman. The leftover liquid swirls around the cup, but the shot is just short of the window. There is no sound when it lands in the tangled, overgrown bushes.

The temperature crawls past one hundred degrees and stays there as the week begins, then drags on, with the sun piercing steadily. The city traps the heat and holds it in the miles of cement. The windless nights do nothing to cool the air.

Carol keeps an eye out for the woman and her red Toyota, but sees neither. One night, stepping out of the shower, she hears Mitch's laugh, then the steady stream of his voice through the open windows. She flicks off the light and stands in the darkness, straining to make sense of his words. She is wet, and when the warm night air circles through the bathroom, she shivers. She sees the trail of phone cord as he paces in front of the stove. It is a relief to find him alone. She dries herself with the damp bath towel in the dark, still listening, trying to figure out who he's talking to.

On Thursday she crosses the front lawn to Mitch's house half an hour before they normally leave for their volunteer jobs. She makes a reference to the heat, saying that she is anxious to be in the air-conditioned library. Mitch is surly, short-tempered. He tells her that he is too hot and too tired to spend another dull evening with Kevin. Carol suggests they go to a movie theater, and Mitch says it's either that or the mall. She wants to bring up the woman but doesn't know how to do it without appearing jealous. Instead, she tells him not to despair. "The heat can't get any worse," she promises.

Donald is standing by the water fountain, and when Carol walks into the library, he gives up his place in line.

"I was thinking about your name," he says.

Carol did not expect him to be there so soon. She is slightly annoyed to see him already.

"Your name is like who you are," Donald continues. "Care. Caring. Carol."

"Oh, really?" Carol plans her dinner with Mitch. Since it is her night to pay, she thinks she will suggest a restaurant where they can order a nice bottle of wine. A place where they can be alone.

"It came to me this weekend when I was practicing reading,"

Donald shows her a piece of paper with her name written across the top. The *O* and the *L* are crossed out and an *E* has been inserted. "You work just like your name. You care about people."

Carol is uncomfortable with this praise. She is just about to change the subject when Donald does.

"I'm learning to read because my wife killed herself." Donald is speaking too fast, and Carol misses the conjunction.

"Excuse me?"

"My wife killed herself last October."

"I'm sorry," Carol says. "That must be difficult. To be alone and all." She makes a vague gesture with her hand as if to include all his sorrow.

"I'm not alone," Donald tells her. "I've got kids. Four kids."

"I'm sure they're a help."

"Sometimes," Donald says. "But mostly they're a drain. A financial drain."

Carol nods in sympathy.

"I couldn't read my wife's suicide note," Donald says.

Carol motions for him to lower his voice. He is not bothering anyone, but she feels that the things he is telling her should be whispered—at least talked about in low tones.

"She left it on the table for Julie to find. That's my oldest, Julie, and she's always the first one home." Donald rips the newspaper article into long thin strips, then shapes them into different-sized spheres that remind Carol of spitballs.

"Did your wife know you couldn't read?" Carol had always assumed that adult illiterates hid the fact that they couldn't read, especially from people close to them. But through the program she had found that there are just as many who are proud of the fact that they can't read. One of her students was arrogant about her illiteracy. The student saw herself as a member of a private club—a club with only a few members and the numbers dwindling.

"Of course she knew I couldn't read. I was married to her, wasn't I?" Donald arranges the newspaper balls in a line and flicks them with a snap of his thumb and index finger. They fly off the table and disappear into the gray carpet—the same color as the newspaper.

Carol puts out her hand to stop Donald from littering in the library, but he thinks she is playing a game and aims directly at her hand as if it were a net.

"That's why she wrote the note," Donald says. "She wanted Julie to read it to me so that I would stop her. She wanted me to get there in time to save her."

Carol does not encourage him by asking about the note, so when Donald explains what happened, she tells herself that it's not her fault. Donald talks the rest of the hour, and even though they have read nothing, when she fills out his progress card she checks the box marked satisfactory improvement.

"It's so sad. Just a sad, sad story." Carol stops talking to sip her wine. "This guy is absolutely devastated and ashamed that he can't read. And talk about a punishment. Nothing as simple as losing a job. He couldn't read his wife's suicide note and didn't give it to anybody in time to save her."

"I don't get it," Mitch says. "How could the wife be so sure that he could have saved her?"

"They own property in Milan, just south of Ann Arbor," Carol explains. "And that's where the wife said she was going to kill herself. Only she didn't drive on the highways. She was scared to death of trucks. She thought they'd stray out of their lanes and smash her car into the guardrails. So when she'd drive out to the property, she'd take the back roads."

"The back roads to Ann Arbor?" Mitch says. "That's got to take a couple of hours."

"Right." Carol tears off a piece of bread and Mitch passes her the butter dish. This small gesture pleases her. It shows her that he is aware of her needs, and she rushes ahead with her story. "That's what the wife was counting on. She thought the daughter would read Donald the note as soon as he got home. Donald would be frantic, and he'd drive out to the property in time to rescue her. But his daughter got sick, and the neighbor across the street came over to borrow something, and Donald forgot all about the note in his pocket."

Mitch asks her if she's going to eat the rest of her chicken. Carol tells him he can have it. She is irritated that he's not more taken with the story. It is just the kind of thing that they usually share about their volunteer jobs.

"His wife was waiting out in the country listening for car tires on the gravel roads. I can just imagine her sitting there on the grass while the sun went down, waiting for someone to save her. I guess when it got dark and no one had come to rescue her, she decided she had to go through with it. Donald thinks it's because no one came that she went ahead and killed herself. She must have gotten lonelier and lonelier, thinking everyone hated her. I mean why else would a whole family ignore a suicide note."

"Did she do it with a gun?" Mitch asks.

"No, she hanged herself."

"That's brutal," Mitch says. "Really brutal."

"I keep thinking about Donald and how guilty he must feel about the whole thing. He says he's embarrassed to go anywhere. He thinks people point at him and say, 'There's that dumb man who couldn't even read his wife's suicide note.'"

"Has he asked you out yet?"

"What are you talking about?"

"It sounds to me like your friend Donald is hitting on you."

"He tells me about his wife killing herself, and you think he's hitting on me?"

"Don't get excited."

"Then tell me what you meant."

"How about if you tell me how much time you spent reading tonight?"

Carol stammers and Mitch laughs.

"See, I told you." Mitch cuts her leftover chicken into squares. "The guy's interested in you."

"He is not interested in me," Carol wipes her mouth and then tosses the napkin onto the table. "He's not like that. He's just a sad man with real problems."

"And you're a young woman willing to listen to him."

"That's right," Carol says. "I'm showing him some compassion."

"An awful lot of compassion from what I can see." Mitch smiles.

"Well, at least it's normal compassion," Carol says.

"What does that mean?"

"He probably doesn't make his women leave the house at six o'clock in the morning."

Mitch drops the fork with the square piece of chicken onto his plate. He is quiet for only a moment. "How long have you been spying on me?"

"I'm not spying on you." The conversation has taken an odd turn, and his anger upsets her. She has no idea how to make herself desirable to this man she wants so desperately.

"What would you call it? Keeping watch on my house?"

"I wasn't watching your house." Carol can feel the perspiration dripping from the backs of her knees onto her calves. She remembers the night in the bathroom, but knows that it would have been impossible for Mitch to see her. "I was reading the newspaper on the porch."

"At six o'clock in the morning? You were out there at six o'clock in the morning?"

"I was up. I wanted to be outside before it got too hot." Her story is true, but her tone is defensive. She shakes her head as if she can physically get rid of this feeling that she has done something wrong.

They are two blocks from home when Carol apologizes. "I'm sorry I upset you." She is not used to admitting that she is wrong, and her words sound awkward.

Mitch nods. "It's me. I'm just hot. Tired, too. Tired of being hot, I guess."

"Me too," Carol agrees.

"Hey. I'm off the hook for next Thursday." Mitch turns down the radio.

"You quit the program?" Carol tries to rid her voice of the tension she feels.

"No, no," Mitch says. "Kevin got sponsored for camp."

"He's going to camp?"

"A CYO camp up in Port Huron," Mitch says. "Right on the lake."

Mitch pulls into his driveway but does not shut off the motor. They talk in the cool of the air-conditioned car. "I don't know what Kevin's going to do in the wilderness. He doesn't seem the type to go into sports or swimming or anything like that."

"That's great," Carol says. In the side mirror she sees their neighbor, Mr. Schott, and his son playing catch. Their shadowy figures move slowly in the fading light.

"I don't know how I'm going to live without my heavy metal video fix," Mitch laughs.

65

"Won't the program want you to take care of another little brother?"

"The kids aren't interchangeable," Mitch explains. "It's not like we're baby-sitters."

"I know that," Carol says. "I just thought they might have someone else who needs a big brother."

"The idea is to form a bond with your little brother," Mitch says. "Not to overload us."

"Donald asked me to do him a favor," Carol says. She had not planned on telling Mitch about Donald's request, but she wants to show him she understands the role of a volunteer worker as much as he does.

"What kind of favor?"

"I guess his wife was in some financial trouble before she killed herself. She wrote a few bad checks that Donald can't make good on right now."

"Is that why she did it?"

"Donald didn't say that," Carol says. "There's this one beautician who keeps calling the house and asking for his wife. Donald can't bring himself to tell the woman that his wife is dead. He asked me to go to the beauty shop and talk to her."

"And you're going to do it?" Mitch asks.

"I think so." Carol nods even though until this moment she had not planned on carrying out the favor. She had told Donald she was in the middle of a busy work week and that she'd let him know.

"You'll have to let me know what happens," Mitch says.

Now Carol has no choice. She must call Donald and tell him that she'll go through with the favor.

"Be careful." Mitch turns the key and they get out of the car. "You know how goofy people can be about money."

66

"Thanks." Carol is touched by his warning. She invites him over for a beer. Mitch suggests another night.

Carol's mood turns sour at his refusal. She wants to ask if that woman is coming over, but she knows it's none of her business.

"Are you sure?" she asks.

"Thanks, anyway," Mitch says. He watches Mr. Schott and his son toss a baseball back and forth. He is calm, clearly unaware how much his casual, non-interested attitude frustrates her.

Carol has never been so forward with a man. Most of the others simply assumed that she was interested in them and took it from there. But with Mitch, she doesn't know what to say to express how she feels. This night she doesn't get a chance. Mr. Schott misses his son's throw, and Mitch runs to retrieve it. The three of them form a triangle and toss the ball back and forth. The rest of the daylight disappears, and soon it is too dark even to see the ball, let alone catch it.

The beauty shop is at the dead end of a one-way street in the center of Ann Arbor. The closest parking structure is full and Carol circles the block three times waiting for someone to leave. Finally she drives down a residential street and parks in the shade of a mountain ash. The shop is a converted Victorian home with window boxes full of geraniums and a white railing up the front steps. Carol tells the receptionist that she'd like to see the manicurist, Pamela. Before she can explain that she doesn't want to have her nails done, the receptionist calls Pamela's name on the intercom system. "There's a walk-in here if you can take her."

Carol starts to explain that she just wants to talk to Pamela, but the phone rings again and the receptionist flips the large pages of the datebook forward. She puts her hand over the receiver.

"You can go on up." She jerks her head to the stairs and then resumes the conversation. It is obvious by the fast pace of her conversation that the person on the other end is not a customer but someone close to the receptionist. Carol climbs the dark-carpeted steps to the second floor, where the hand-printed sign directs her to Pamela's table. Pamela stands up from her manicure stand and asks Carol to take off her rings and watch.

"We give hand massages here," she explains. "You don't want any metal on your body."

Carol slips off her jewelry and sets it next to the dish of soapy water. She feels intimidated by Pamela's looks. Her hair is wound tight on top of her head, and her hands and makeup are perfect. Nothing is out of place, and Carol feels underdressed, more like a tomboy in her jeans and faded button-down.

Pamela examines her hands, picking the loose skin with a pair of tiny silver scissors.

"I don't usually get manicures." Carol feels she must explain why she is here. "Except if I'm in someone's wedding."

"Your nails are strong," Pamela says, not looking up, "but you've got bad cuticles. You shouldn't pick at them."

"I actually came to see you about a friend of mine," Carol says. "Donald Rice."

"I don't have many men customers," Pamela tells her. "Men who live in big cities get their nails done, but here in Ann Arbor, we really only get women."

"His wife was a client," Carol explains. Pamela places her right hand in a dish of warm soapy water. "Do you remember Evelyn Rice?"

"That woman owes me money." Pamela wipes her hands on the folded white towel and then flips open the drawer.

"Yes, I know."

"She owes me fifty-two dollars." She shows Carol her ledger, full of numbers and red marks. She points to Evelyn's name in the left column.

"She won't return my phone calls." Pamela puts the book away. "I call her almost every day, and her husband just beats around the bush about paying me back."

Pamela begins digging under Carol's left nail with a long toothpick-type instrument. It pinches Carol's skin and she pulls away.

"Listen. You tell her that I have to pay rent on this booth. You tell her I want my money. I can't afford to have people bounce checks on me."

"She's dead," Carol says. "That's what I came here to tell you. Evelyn Rice killed herself last October."

Pamela looks at her in surprise. "Dead?"

Carol nods. A strong chemical smell stings her nostrils, and Carol lifts her hand from the soapy dishwater and rubs her nose.

"Perming solution," Pamela explains, then asks. "Are you related?"

"I'm his reading teacher," Carol explains. "I volunteer at the local library."

"Then why'd he send you in to do his dirty work? Why can't he just call me and tell me what happened? He could have told me his wife was dead. I've talked to him on the phone almost every week. I'm a person. I've got sympathy."

"I think he was afraid," Carol says. "He was afraid to tell you the truth." Though they are talking about Donald, she can't help but think of Mitch. She wishes he were here to help explain the situation.

Pamela spreads yellow lotion on Carol's hands and massages it the length of her arm to her elbows. She circles her fingers around Carol's wrists until the moisturizer disappears. It smells of cucumbers. The room is air-conditioned, and Carol feels comfortable with this woman massaging her arms. She is so relaxed that she closes her eyes.

"All I was trying to do was collect my money," Pamela says. "I didn't mean to call a dead woman's house." She shivers as if superstitious. "That poor, poor man. And here's me calling him about some manicure payment."

Carol gets home just as Mitch pulls into his driveway. They get out of their cars simultaneously. Carol waves and walks over, full of the story of Ann Arbor and the beauty shop. The sun is bright, and she does not see the passenger door open until she is just up to the car. Carol gets flustered immediately. She starts to retreat, but then feels foolish, as if she has done something wrong.

"I wanted to tell you about Pamela," Carol speaks directly to Mitch, ignoring the woman as best she can.

"What?" Mitch closes the car door and stands in the street waiting for her to explain.

"Donald's favor," Carol holds her fingers stiff, though by now the polish must surely be dry. "It was a little more than I expected."

"Everything okay?" Mitch asks.

"Yeah. I guess so." She hesitates, then decides that this is not a good time. It occurs to her that there might never be a good time, that maybe the only choice she has is to give up on Mitch. "I'll give you the details later."

"Remember you're only the guy's reading teacher," Mitch warns. He smiles and looks concerned. "Don't get too involved."

"Oh, no," Carol says. She flips her hands around and holds them so Mitch can see the color. Dark mauve. Her nails have never looked so good. Although it does not seem to matter too much right now.

As they had agreed, Carol meets Donald at the restaurant around the corner from her house. She picked a place that would be bright, loud, full of people. The afternoon is hot, the heat has returned as forcefully as it has all summer. It is not quite two o'clock when Carol pushes open the glass door of Costanzo's and sees Donald sitting in the second booth from the window with a pitcher of beer and two mugs. He stands and shakes her hand and thanks her for being on time.

"You're a very caring person." He pours her mug full of foamy beer.

Carol does not usually drink during the day, but she is thirsty and warm from the walk over.

"Did you talk with the girl?" Donald asks as soon as she's had a sip.

"Yes," Carol says. The beer is cold, and she drinks in long swallows. Donald refills her glass.

"And?"

"And she's beautiful," Carol says. "She wants to be a model."

"My wife never talked about the beauty parlor." Donald's tongue slides awkwardly over the last words as if he is not used to saying these kinds of things.

"She's saving all her money to get into an agency," Carol explains. She remembers exactly what Pamela was doing with the nail file, then the cream, then the polish when she talked with Carol. "That's why she can't afford bounced checks. She's trying to earn her own way into this agency so they can get her photo work."

"Did you tell her about my wife?"

"She's real sorry," Carol says. Donald fills her half-empty mug. "She said to tell you she's real sorry."

"What about the check?"

"Because of what's happened and all, she says not to worry about the money," Carol says. "She's a very fair person."

Donald claps his hands as if applauding her actions. "That's so good," he says. "That's just great. How am I going to pay you back?"

"I was glad to help." Carol giggles when the foam fizzles into her nose.

Donald keeps nodding his head, giving her his approval. "You didn't mind doing it?" he asks.

"It was fine."

"My wife left me with a financial mess when she died."

The bartender flips on the television, and Carol turns to look at the images on the oversized screen.

"She wrote checks to just about everybody in this area," Donald says. "I wonder if you could help me with another favor?"

"What's that?" The beer is slowing her reactions, and she doesn't hear him.

"Do you think you could talk to some other people who are bothering me?"

"Collect on another bounced check?" Carol asks. "I don't think so."

Donald sits back in his seat. Carol focuses on the television. It is a baseball game. Probably the Tigers, but she cannot be sure.

"Why not?"

"Because," Carol says repeating Mitch's words, which somehow seem right, "I'm your reading teacher. I'm supposed to be helping you learn to read."

"But I need other help," Donald says. "That's what you're involved in. Doing charity work."

"To help you read," Carol reminds him.

"I needed to read before my wife committed suicide,"

Donald says. "Now I need help clearing her debts. This is the kind of help I need now."

"I don't know," Carol says. She feels too guilty simply to refuse, but she knows that her whole reason for volunteering was wrong. It was not to help anyone but herself. She feels selfish and stupid and terribly alone. Donald is obviously disappointed when she tells him that she'll think about doing the favor.

Carol has rarely been drunk in the middle of the day, and the buzz in her head feels like bursts of wild energy, though a minute later she is exhausted. Yesterday's unopened mail is spread out on the couch, and she sits down and begins tearing at the envelopes. The mail is mostly bills. She throws the extra envelopes and perfumed advertisements into a pile before letting all the paper fall to the floor.

The afternoon gets warmer and the streets get quieter, as if the whole neighborhood is sleeping through the heat. Carol is sweating before she wakes up. She can smell the beer on her skin, and the dizziness she felt before her nap is gone as if she has sweated all the alcohol from her body. It takes Carol a few minutes to recognize where she is, and another minute before she remembers what day it is.

After a shower, Carol looks through her oversized purse for her hairbrush and realizes she can't find her wallet. She dumps everything onto the kitchen counter, then remembers taking it out at the restaurant. She knows she's left it on the dark-red cushioned booth at Costanzo's restaurant.

The bar is crowded now. The noise level has increased, and the change in lights makes the place look different—not at all like the place where she drank five glasses of beer. She is dehydrated, and when the bartender asks if he can get her something, Carol cannot speak. He pours a glass of water and she drinks it down before she tells him about her wallet. She starts to identify it—gray with a large silver buckle clasp—when he sets it on the bar in front of her.

"We didn't have a phone number on you," he apologizes. "But we figured you might come looking for it."

Carol opens the wallet and checks for her credit cards and driver's license. Everything is there, even the cash.

She hears Donald a minute before she actually sees him at the side table with a woman. She recognizes the pleading tone of his voice and his words, so carefully chosen.

"I'm afraid to tell anyone about my situation," Donald says. "I know people point at me and think, 'There's that stupid man who couldn't read his wife's suicide note.' You should have seen it at the funeral. I couldn't stand all the pity people felt for me. Even from my own kids. I've got four of them."

"I'm so sorry." The woman nods in sympathy.

"There are plenty of problems to deal with when your wife commits suicide," Donald says and the woman keeps nodding in sympathy and agreement.

All of a sudden, Carol understands what Donald is up to. She sees how he does it, how he manipulates people into doing things for him. She realizes that what she is feeling is admiration. She admires how easily Donald gets people to do things for him. All he does is make it clear to them what he wants. It's that simple. He tells people what he needs and people help him. Now she must spell it out for Mitch.

The mower is in the middle of the garage. She does not need the light to see the silver metal shining in the glow of the street lamps. She drags it backward to the edge of Mitch's property and then runs her hand down the side of the machine to find the starter. She pulls the cord and the power kicks as she lets it slide back in. She starts out slowly while her muscles adjust to the vibration and the weight of the machine.

At nine o'clock the night air is full of shadows. The smell of cut grass rises from the ground, a surprising freshness so late in the day. She moves horizontally, getting closer to his house as she finishes each strip. She cannot see her rows and tries to keep the machine as straight as possible. Mitch comes out and watches from the front porch. She waves, the motor vibrating under her arms. He is saying something. She can hear him shouting, but not his words.

He moves his hand across his throat in quick jerky motions, telling her to cut the engine.

"What are you doing?" She shuts off the machine and his words tear through the neighborhood in the sudden silence.

"I'm showing you I care," she says. "I'm showing you that I care about you."

"What do you mean you care about me?" He looks puzzled, as if he thinks she's gone crazy.

"I'm showing you that I want something more," she says with force.

"You don't have to cut my lawn," he says.

"I've got to do something," Carol says. "That's all I know. I've just got to do something."

Carol pulls the cord. The machine jumps and then starts. The shadows are too deep for her to see his expression, but she imagines it to be one of confusion. She knows she must get rid of this. She must make it clear to Mitch that she cares for him. She takes a deep breath and then, pushing on the long metal handle with all her strength, moves forward toward the edge of the lawn. Mitch follows. If not totally understanding what she is doing, he is at least right there beside her.

Moving Miami

SOMEONE COMPARED THE PROBLEMS Marybeth, Doug, and Marco went through last year to dominoes falling—one thing setting off the next—until everything was too much of a mess to pick up. Why the whole thing started was a bit harder to figure out. There were those who thought it was Doug's fault. He was stupid to let Marco move in so soon after the wedding. Other people thought Marco was a jerk. There was just no excuse for sleeping with your best friend's wife.

Most everyone, though, blamed Marybeth. They never actually called her a slut, but they found other words: attention deficit disorder as it applied to the marital bed, low self-esteem as it applied to her own sense of honor, and quack as it applied to—well, everyone knew what that applied to. Still, no one can expect interest in a failing marriage to last longer than the marriage itself, and gossip about the trio faded as the summer came to an end. By the time Hurricane Andrew slammed into Miami, destroying everything in sight, people were talking of other things. The affair seemed far away, as if it had happened years ago to another group of friends in some distant city.

Marybeth and Doug met at Biscayne Baby, a Coconut Grove nightclub, on Doug's twenty-ninth birthday. Doug and his friends arrived after midnight and immediately began playing a game they used to play in college when drinking funds were hard to come by. Money was no longer an issue, but it was still fun to see if they could get away with it. They'd look for a group of single girls, although this was not always easy to tell in a crowded club. They'd talk them up, ask them to dance. Once they were on the floor, the others would make a grab for the girls' drinks. The women drank strawberry daiquiris, piña coladas, and something blended with grapefruit juice and rum and grenadine. Doug, buzzed from the sugar, quit after a couple of rounds and stood at the far end of the bar watching his friends on the dance floor. The strobe lights were flashing to the beat of the music, and he closed his eyes until the dizziness faded.

Marybeth was bartending that night, and though she did not know these guys personally, she could see exactly what they were up to. She thought they were too old to be playing such a stupid game, so when Doug ordered a glass of ice water, she charged him a hundred dollars. No one had complained—the girls didn't seem to realize what was going on—but she thought they were being rude. Ridiculously cheap. Doug only had twenty dollars on him. He gave Marybeth one of his business cards and promised to come back the next night with the rest of the cash. He forgot his promise, but a few days later Marybeth called his office and asked if he wanted to drive to Ft. Lauderdale to see the hydroplane races. Doug agreed, hoping she wouldn't ask him for the money he owed her. They left Miami before noon with a picnic lunch and a Styrofoam cooler full of Very Berry White Wine Spritzers. Strong winds delayed the race, finally canceling it. Still, it was a beautiful day, and rather than getting right back in the slow-moving highway traffic, Marybeth and Doug spent the afternoon on the beach.

Marybeth wouldn't take off her tennis shoes, and when Doug asked her what she was afraid of, she told him that her right foot was webbed. The skin between her toes was almost transparent, but it was obvious that her toes were connected, and she was self-conscious about showing people. The kids in grade school used to quack at her on the playground. They'd move their arms up and down like they had two short wings and sing a song about rubber ducks. She never got used to having a deformed foot. She refused to show it to Doug when he asked if he could see it. It was too early in the relationship, she teased, but he was touched that she had told him about it.

They dated steadily for the next three or four months, then agreed not to see other people, though sometimes when Doug said he had soccer practice he took out his next-door neighbor for barbecued ribs. She was a sad but striking woman who became weepy when she drank. She was often crying when the waiter brought their coffee and wet-naps, and the only advice Doug could give her was to tell her that things couldn't be as bad as they seemed. She said he was living in a dream world. Real people hurt. Real people were dying of loneliness. Doug made out with her on his living room couch before walking her home. But when she pressed him about her ideas, he admitted that he didn't understand what she wanted him to do about it all. As far as he was concerned, there was nothing he could do.

Biscayne Baby closed soon after they started dating, so Marybeth went back to nursing. A retirement home in Miami Beach hired her from a telephone interview. She actually preferred bartending to nursing, but club hours were tough in Miami—most places stayed open until 3 or 4 A.M. Afterward she would have clean-up cocktails with her co-workers, and it would be morning by the time she drove home. It felt strange to be caught in rush-hour traffic, her uniform smelling of alcohol and cigarettes. Doug was relieved when she quit working there. Too many guys hung out at those places. There were too many single guys looking for someone like Marybeth.

Their wedding was a Hawaiian-style pig roast at the public park in Coconut Grove. Their friends came dressed in loud printed shirts, khaki shorts, sandals. A few people wore nothing but bathing suits. Doug and Marybeth passed out leis in the reception line. The reggae band seemingly played "Red, Red Wine" over and over—the same for hours. Marybeth thought a song about a guy trying to forget a former lover was an odd choice for a wedding reception, but the dance floor stayed crowded all night, and their friends all agreed that it was the best wedding they had ever been to.

Marybeth and Doug bought a condo on Key Biscayne—where everyone assumed they were living happily enough—until early May when Doug's best friend, Marco, moved into their spare bedroom. Marco's girlfriend had been a pilot for Eastern Airlines, but when the company began major layoffs, she started looking for other jobs. She had no intention of giving up her accumulated flying hours just to stay in Miami, a city she had grown up in but had never particularly liked. The highways were always under construction, and when they weren't they were still confusing. Even using the ocean as a permanent marker, she couldn't figure out which way she was going. She often found herself by the airport when she wanted to be on the beach.

"How can you navigate a plane, but not be able to get from point A to point B on the ground?" Marco asked her.

"Miami's outgrown itself," was all she would say. "It's no longer interesting." When USAir offered her a position in Pittsburgh, she took the promotion and the transfer with no qualms about leaving Miami.

They talked about Marco moving to Pittsburgh, but she wanted to get married and he wouldn't—or, rather, couldn't— do it. He loved her, but not enough to marry her. She was a woman who worked long hours in a high-stress job. On her nonflying days she liked to sit in the sun and read mystery novels. She had a short attention span and liked bars with pool tables. She drank beer straight from the bottle and ate vegetables without washing them first. Marco refused to talk with her about buying property on the Carolina shoreline because he sensed she was thinking about building a retirement home, and he didn't like the idea of knowing where he was going to end up before he had celebrated his thirtieth birthday. Marco offered to help her haul her stuff to Pittsburgh, but she told him not to be ridiculous. The company would pay for a professional mover. When the lease on her apartment ran out, she went north to stay with some college friends. Over the weekend, the moving van came and hauled her things away. Marco was left in Miami without a place to stay.

He had been having financial problems since March, when he and ten other employees went through what the *Miami Herald* called a "schedule adjustment." It meant that they were laid off, maybe fired, but definitely collecting unemployment.

Marco had been one of the sports photographers. He covered Class A minor high school sports—soccer, tennis, fencing, swimming meets. He also did local stories—third-generation coaches in the Upper Keys, Miami rugby players who practiced by dragging tractor tires on the beach. He had tried to get the job as the Miami Heat photographer, but the paper hired a woman from the *Detroit Free Press* who had covered the Pistons' two NBA championship seasons. The sports editor promised Marco that he was first in line for the Florida Marlins job when the *Herald* started its "schedule adjustments."

The same week as the schedule adjustments, his car was stolen from the Taurus Restaurant parking lot. It was during a Friday afternoon happy hour, with at least forty people on the outdoor patio. Marco found it hard to believe that no one had seen anything. The valet, a tall, lanky kid with a missing front tooth, claimed to have been helping the busboys carry garbage out to the dumpsters when the thieves jumped the fence, smashed the window, and hot-wired Marco's car.

Marco filed a report, and the police insisted on coming out to see the spot where the car had been. There was nothing there, just the empty parking space, but the policeman knelt and inspected the blacktop as if looking for clues.

"Dade County gravel." The policeman scooped up some of the broken glass and held it up for Marco's inspection. He seemed particularly pleased by the tiny glass slivers.

"Any chance I'll get the car back?" Marco asked.

"About a zillion to one." The cop shone his flashlight into the dark bushes. There was a pile of empty beer bottles and some Burger King wrappers. He made notes on a yellow pad of paper that Marco was sure he tossed in the garbage dumpsters before driving away.

"Your car is probably sleeping in Puerto Rico as we speak," the policeman told Marco. "Tomorrow morning, those car parts will be all over the country."

"Are you sure?" Marco asked, though he had worked at the newspaper long enough to know what happened to stolen cars in Miami.

"Positive," the guy said and then told Marco not to worry. "That's why we pay through the nose for insurance."

Marco had meant to reinstate his policy ever since it had run out last November, but the first few times he called the company he was put on hold. Not crazy about Muzak, he hung up and tried again, only to get a busy signal. Then it was Christmas break, then New Year's, Valentine's Day, a presidential long weekend. Then he lost his job.

Marco liked living with Marybeth and Doug. They were only the second tenants to occupy their place, and every room smelled of paint and new carpeting. Marco's bedroom looked out on the courtyard and the grove of ficus trees that blocked the noise of traffic. But with no car and Doug at work all day, Marco got bored. He missed his old girlfriend, who was lazy about returning his phone calls. When she did call, she talked about Pittsburgh. She liked landing planes over the rolling Allegheny Mountains and looked forward to the opening of the new airport in October. She did not invite Marco north even when he hinted that he'd like to see her.

Marybeth quit nursing at the retirement home to study for her GMAT right about the time Marco moved into the apartment. She had been unhappy working there and wanted to do something different with her life. Everyone she talked to suggested business. With her medical background and an MBA degree, lots of doors would be open to her. Besides studying for her graduate exam, she was using the time off work to have the toes on her right foot un-webbed. She had wanted to do something about her foot ever since she could remember, and Doug agreed. It was ridiculous to walk around with something that could be so easily changed. The operation was cosmetic, but she had never been able to afford it until she married Doug.

The procedure was not very complicated. It consisted of a series of operations to tear away the skin between the individual toes. Her foot was too sore to put weight on and walking was painful. Doug had an old pair of crutches, and she tried using them, but they were too tall and dug into her underarms. She spent most of her time on the couch with her study guides open on her lap. She flipped through them without reading a word and made doodles in the margins with the pencils she sharpened with her eyeliner sharpener. She was afraid that if she watched TV she'd get addicted to afternoon soap operas. Instead, she listened to the radio. She called in when they announced contests and tried to win prizes. She was the sixth caller once. The station was giving away front-row tickets to the U2 concert to the seventh caller, but the disc jockey took her song request and played it a half hour after her call.

Marco was afraid Marybeth would get tired of seeing him all the time, so he tried not to bother her. Job hunting was tough—no one was hiring—but he made a few calls every morning. Mostly he called friends, who loved to talk but couldn't help him connect with a job. They planned their evening workouts and gossiped like guys do, as if everything they're talking about is business.

With no income, Marco couldn't go anywhere except to the gym, where his job at the *Herald* had guaranteed him a lifetime membership. Mornings he spent at the pool. Built right in the center of the condominium complex, the kidney-shaped pool was surrounded by trees that shed tiny red berries on the lounge chairs. A woman and her two kids were always there. No matter how early Marco got up, the three of them would be there before him. The kids had neon-colored floats and played a stupid game called Marco Polo. There were only two of them—one kept his eyes closed and called out Marco, the other was supposed to answer. Hearing his own name was irritating, as was their cheating. One didn't keep his eyes closed and the other pretended to be underwater and didn't answer. They splashed water everywhere and never got tired. The mother—perhaps she was the baby-sitter—napped all morning long. Their screaming didn't seem to bother her, and she seemed just as oblivious to the red stains the berries were making on the backs of her thighs.

After an hour at the pool, Marco would take a walk around the neighborhood. The Key Biscayne library had odd summer hours that he could never keep straight, but the librarian had once asked him if he was one of the boat people, and Marco, misunderstanding her question, answered yes. She issued him a marina library card for people who had boats in the bay. Books wrapped in plastic covers could be checked out for two months at a time.

Marybeth was bored out of her mind. She flunked every single one of the practice exams and figured she wasn't business school material. She thought about going back to her nursing job, but when she called the retirement home, they said they wouldn't need her until September.

She started going through the *Miami Herald* every morning, when Marco was finished with it. She carefully crossed out the jobs she had already called about or the ones she wasn't qualified or wouldn't take. There weren't many options, and Marco kidded her about not calling up the "dancers with good attitude wanted" numbers. The ads never said topless or nude, but they said they were looking for women interested in fun and adventures.

"Would you ever consider doing something like that?" Marco asked. Marco worked out a few mornings a week in the gym, and his body smelled of the weight room—like steel.

"I used to work in a bar," Marybeth said. "Never topless, but I thought it was a great way to make money." She was suddenly anxious to be doing something besides sitting around the apartment.

"I remember," Marco said. "I was there the night Doug met you."

"Really?" Marybeth asked.

"Shows you what an impression I make on women," Marco said, though he did not believe this. He thought women paid an awful lot of attention to him. He had always been pleased with the way women noticed him.

"You were probably too drunk to remember me," Marybeth said. It didn't feel like they were flirting, but she was aware that Marco was looking at her, and she wondered what he saw. The operations had made her tired. She rarely bothered to put on anything besides a T-shirt and a pair of shorts.

"Not as drunk as Rodney," Marco said. "He threw up that coconut crap from those piña coladas for days."

"If he had paid for his own drinks, he wouldn't have been so sick." Marybeth was not a firm believer in karma, but there were times when she thought she understood how it worked.

Marybeth's toes were completely independent of each other, but the operation had changed nothing in her life. She hadn't expected a miracle, but she had thought something would have changed. Her foot ached. She rubbed tiger balm around her toes, but the dull pain was always there. Marybeth was allergic to narcotics, so Marco suggested she drink.

"A glass of wine might help you relax," he told her. She could not find the corkscrew, so they split a can of beer and played a game of cribbage. They finished the beers in the refrigerator and, after a while, her foot did feel better. She no longer felt any pain.

When Marco asked her if she wanted some time to study, she told him that she had given up the idea of getting an MBA. They went to lunch at the Mexican restaurant on Key Biscayne. It was a slow time of the day to be there—the waitresses were filling salt and pepper shakers, the bartender was watching soap operas. They ordered nachos and margaritas and discussed their dream jobs. Marybeth's idea of a great way to earn money had something to do with clothes and glamorous people. No, she didn't want to be a model, but she wouldn't mind working on commercials. Marco confided that he had always wanted to be a deep-sea diver, then blushed, knowing this was a lie. He was terrified of the ocean. Like jumping from an airplane, deep-sea diving was something he liked to watch in movies but had no desire to try himself. I'm talking her up, Marco thought. I'm talking up my best friend's wife.

"I've always hated swimming," Marybeth said. "Because of my toes. I was afraid that people would look at me and think I was a duck or something." She did not tell him about the fourth-graders on the playground, but he said he understood how cruel people could be.

He asked if he could see her foot and she said no, but after a third round of margaritas, when her tongue was heavy with salt, she pulled off her too-big sandal—the one she bought for sixty-nine cents at the drugstore—and pulled her knee up to the table. Marco leaned across the booth to have a look, and his right hand knocked the margarita into her lap. The blended drink was cold against her bare legs; she let out a short screech. Marco apologized and went up to the bar for some rags to clean it up. Her shirt was soaked, and they left the restaurant so she could change into something dry. The streets were empty. They walked down by the marina—the long way home. It was too calm and warm for sailing and the boats were tied up, the sheets clinking against the sailing shafts. The air was heavy with heat, but they sat at the end of the dock with their feet dangling into the mosquito-infested water until the sun and the margaritas gave them a headache. When Doug came home from work he found them both asleep—Marybeth in the bedroom with the air conditioner on high, Marco on the couch using the want ads as a pillow.

Doug and Marco were jogging when Marco asked how Doug felt about Marybeth giving up on business school.

"What's this?" Doug asked.

"Marybeth," Marco said. "Her change of heart about business school?"

"That's a surprise to me," Doug said. It was almost midnight—the only time to exercise outdoors in Miami—but the heat was still making it difficult to breathe. Marco made a noise in his throat and this made him cough, which tired him further.

"Did she say something to you?" Doug asked.

"No," Marco exhaled. He didn't have to pretend to be having problems with his breathing—he thought he was going to faint from lack of air.

"Has she quit studying?"

"I don't know," Marco said.

"You must know something," Doug said. "The two of you are there in the condo every day."

They were at the water's edge. The ocean smelled of gasoline. Marco slowed down, then stopped altogether. Doug jogged in a tight circle around him.

"You go back, buddy," Marco told him. "I'm beat."

"You're stronger than this heat," Doug coaxed his friend without much enthusiasm.

"Not tonight," Marco said and bent over to rub his calves. "I'm dogged to the bones." His muscles were stiff and his body felt heavy, as if he were running with ankle weights.

Doug, a much better runner, was glad to leave Marco behind. He short-cutted along Sonesta Beach and down by the Sheraton. A few people were sitting on the outdoor balcony, but most were inside in the comfort of the air-conditioned bars. He ran quickly—it felt good to move at his own pace.

Marybeth had just turned off the news when Doug came bursting into the apartment. It was the third time she had watched the news that day.

"What is it that makes you tell him things before you find the time to mention them to me?" Marybeth, thinking Marco was in the condo, asked Doug to close the door.

"Is there something going on that I should know about?" Doug slammed the door.

"Of course not," Marybeth said but her heart began beating and she felt slightly dizzy. She sat on the edge of the bed, refusing to look at her husband. He asked her if they were sleeping together, and she said no. "I wouldn't cheat on you," she promised.

"He's my best friend," Doug said.

"I know who he is," Marybeth said.

Doug's running shorts were soaked with sweat, and the steady cold air from the air conditioner made him shiver. She told him to take a shower before he got sick. They continued fighting when he came out of the shower. He had wrapped himself in three towels—something that irritated Marybeth—but Doug pointed out that they had a washer and dryer two feet from their bedroom. If he wanted to use all the towels in the world, he could. He was paying for that luxury. They made up before going to bed but did not make love.

The next day Marco asked her what they had been fighting about. He knew, of course. The walls in the condo weren't soundproof, especially when he cupped his hand around his ear.

"He thinks we're having an affair."

"He's fighting about us?" Marco asked, and Marybeth nodded.

Marco and Doug had known each other since before they were born. Their mothers were best friends who had met on a high school double date when they went on a Sea-Escape cruise to the Bahamas. The memory of that night still made their mothers laugh—it had something to do with one of the passengers jumping overboard and his friends not reporting it until they were in Freeport—a fact that seemed to bond the women. They were still close, close friends.

"He should trust me." Marco crossed his legs. She could see the darker leg hairs on the insides of his thighs. "Especially with his wife."

"What does that mean?" Marybeth asked.

Marco was eating a mango. It was too ripe, and he had turned the skin inside out. The juice ran down his chin, and he licked himself like a cat.

"Especially with his wife?" Marybeth said. "What does that

mean?" She went to the kitchen and pulled down a section of paper towel. Her swift movements pulled the roll away from the wall.

"I mean if you were just his girlfriend that'd be something different," Marco explained when she sat back down. "But you guys are legal and all."

She handed him the paper toweling, and he wrapped the mango in it and wiped his chin with his T-shirt. He had jumped into the pool on his way back from the gym and his T-shirt was damp from his wet suit. The white cotton was stained slightly orange.

"He should trust us," Marybeth said. But she did not trust herself, and two days later, it was Marybeth who made the first move. They made love on the living room floor with the radio tuned to a talk show about the upcoming presidential election. They continued commenting on the program while they were having sex, as if they could ignore what they were doing. Afterward, Marybeth was so filled with guilt and dread that she almost called Doug at work and told him what had happened. It would have been such a relief if she could call, confess, and be forgiven. She wasn't used to having secrets from Doug, and she wasn't pleased with the secret she had now.

That night she was too nervous to face him and faked a headache. She went to bed before he got home. Marco was somewhere—she didn't ask where he was going. Doug did.

"The gym," Marybeth lied. "I think he said he was going to the gym."

Doug went into Marco's room. She heard him click on the light. A minute later he clicked it off. "His workout bag is there," Doug told her. "He wouldn't go to the gym without his workout bag."

"I don't know," Marybeth said. She didn't have to open her

eyes to know that Doug was looking at her. She turned to the wall and pulled the sheet over her head.

The next morning Marybeth got up before Doug. She made him breakfast and then went out to the pool with the morning paper after Doug left for work. She pulled a red-spotted lawn chair into the deep shade of the ficus trees and sat there staring at the sky. It was hot and she would have preferred to be inside with the air conditioner, but the apartment reminded her that she had cheated on her husband.

"That's it," she told herself. "I won't do it again." But Marco came out sometime before ten o'clock and asked her if she was upset.

"No," she said and shook her head.

They were silent until she suggested a swim. The water was too warm, and the dull film on top of it kept them from diving, but they stood in the shallow end, where they moved around slowly. Their hipbones touched once and Marybeth reached out to steady herself. Marco put his arms around her waist and they began to kiss. She did not tell him that the stucco wall was biting into her legs or that the water made her un-webbed foot feel weightless.

Marco pulled down the straps of her bikini top and kissed her throat. Marybeth told herself that since they had already slept together once, there was no reason not to do it again. The woman and her two kids were there. They were staring at Marybeth and Marco, not at all embarrassed by their own curiosity.

Marybeth had no answer when she asked herself why she was cheating on Doug. She was not a stupid woman. She knew sleeping with Marco was wrong. She knew that it would hurt Doug if he found out. She was bored, she reasoned. The days were long, her foot hurt, there was nothing to do, and Marco was there. He was there, all the time, every day. Instead of the soap operas she had vowed to stay away from, she was addicted to sleeping with Marco.

The goalie on Doug's soccer team wasn't the only one to see Marco and Marybeth together, but he was the first to tell Doug.

"Where?" was what Doug asked.

"Señor Frogs," the goalie told him. "They were in the back booth, kissing. Eating tortilla chips and guacamole dip, but mostly kissing."

"Are you sure it was them?"

"It was the middle of the afternoon," the goalie said. "They didn't act like they were hiding anything."

Marco and Marybeth were betting quarters on the final *Jeopardy* question when Doug got home that night. He walked in, kicked over the coffee table, and told them he never wanted to see them again. The ashtray holding their coins flipped onto the floor. Marybeth, wanting to be busy, knelt forward and began picking them up. Her foot bent under itself and she cried out in pain. It was a mistake. Her cry made Doug look at her, and he took the expression on her face to be one of pained guilt.

"I want you out of here by tomorrow morning," Doug shouted at them. "Out."

Neither Marco nor Marybeth asked him what he was talking about. They did not ask him how he found out about their affair, and Doug didn't ask them any questions.

"Everything," Doug said before he went in the bedroom and slammed the door. "All your shit."

Marybeth's stare was fixed on the carpet. Her heart was

pounding and she thought she was going to be sick. Doug came out of the bedroom once more and told them again that he wanted them gone, ASAP. No questions, no answers, no explanations, he just wanted them out of his sight.

Marybeth agreed that Marco should move, but she felt she deserved forgiveness. She was sorry for what she had done. It had been stupid and wrong. She thought she could get Doug to understand, but he refused to speak to her. Marco moved into his brother's place, a small house in Coconut Grove, and when Marybeth understood that Doug's silent treatment was going to last as long as she was in the apartment, she went over and moved in with Marco and his brother.

Marco's brother had been bitten by a shark two years earlier when he was snorkeling in the Bahamas, and his house was filled with sharks and things that looked like sharks—pot holders, bookends, rubber rafts for the pool. The scar was bright red—the hair on his calf no longer grew. Marybeth showed him her toes and they talked about how much their scars itched when it rained. She knew he wasn't thrilled with their being there, and she tried to make herself useful around the house. She cleaned and polished the floors and did the dishes until Marco's brother found her on her knees scrubbing the toilet bowl. "I hire someone to do that," he told her. He was polite enough, but she caught a hint of sarcasm in his tone. "They come in once a week and get paid to do that."

The school year was about to start, and even in south Florida there was a slight change in temperature that told people the rainy season was over—it was almost fall. Marco felt the rush he used to get in college when classes started up every year. September meant sports, and he wanted to be out taking photographs.

Marybeth's period was late. She did not think she was pregnant, but she told Marco that something might be up.

"It's not mine," Marco said in a way that reminded her of a high school boy she had approached with the same kind of news. "In case you haven't noticed, I've always used a condom. Your husband doesn't."

"They're not 100 percent," Marybeth said. She felt cranky and heavy and knew that she was probably going to start her period soon. She was unhappy with Marco and did not want to be living with him. She knew she should leave, but she wasn't sure where she wanted to go.

Marco was caught by surprise every time he walked in the house and saw Marybeth sitting on the couch. He never got used to being with her. Mostly, though, he missed Doug. He couldn't stand not talking to him.

His life was not something he recognized anymore. Once he had lived with an ambitious woman. He himself had once been ambitious. Now he felt like a slug. Lazy, no direction, no savings—he was ashamed of the way he was living. He did not even have enough money to go into the Grove and buy a nice meal.

One afternoon he stopped by Doug's condo on Key Biscayne with a six-pack of beer. He was so nervous that he could feel the sweat beads running down the backs of his legs. He stuttered when he said hello and stood outside apologizing for coming over. Doug acted as if Marco's visit was the most natural thing in the world. He took the beer, complained that it was cheap, that it was too warm to drink, then suggested that they go out and get something to drink.

They drove to the sports bar on the edge of Coconut Grove where a couple of Doug's soccer buddies were watching an Olympic basketball game on the big screen. They called Marco a wimp. They didn't mention Marybeth. This was how they talked when they were drunk, and Marco agreed with them— he was a wimp. He bought a round of Heinekens and after the game they threw darts for a couple of hours. By midnight they were too drunk to drive and rather than call a cab, they decided to walk.

Halfway home, Marco began to cry. Apologizing, but mostly crying, he repeated over and over how he had ruined their friendship. Under the bright lights of the EasyKwik liquor store, Doug stopped and punched Marco in the face.

"You ruined my marriage," Doug reminded him. "What the fuck were you thinking?"

"I wasn't," Marco said. "I wasn't thinking at all." Doug punched him again.

Marco's nose was broken, but the doctor at the Coral Gables Emergency Clinic wouldn't treat Marco until he sobered up, so Doug and Marco spent the rest of night on the bench outside the hospital. The sliding glass doors kept opening, throwing light onto the sidewalk, and neither of them slept. The next day Marco moved his things over to Doug's. He still didn't have a car, and he didn't want to ask anyone for help. The afternoon was warm, and his bags were difficult to carry. He stopped at every street corner, as if obeying the stop signs, to catch his breath. The brown shopping bags were ripping. A kid on a bicycle rode past and Marco called out and asked him for help. He promised him five dollars if he helped him get his things over to Key Biscayne. The kid agreed, but when they got to the condo, Marco realized he didn't have any cash. The six-pack of beer was still in the refrigerator and Marco gave him that instead.

Marybeth's stay at Marco's brother's became awkward after Marco left. She knew she should leave; she should never have moved in.

Her best friend lived with her boyfriend in a small apartment in Coral Gables. They had terrazzo floors that smelled of mildew, and she told herself she was waiting for another plan, anything to avoid going there.

Some people thought Marybeth would start something with Marco's brother. She certainly didn't seem to be picky. But Marco's brother was dating a second-semester freshman from the University of Miami. A tall, blond girl, she was the ninth or tenth alternate on the U.S. Olympic diving team. She didn't make the cut for Barcelona, but she was only eighteen years old and Atlanta in '96 was something to look forward to.

Marybeth slept until ten o'clock most mornings. She was not tired, but she wanted to avoid Marco's brother. She couldn't, however, avoid the note he left on the kitchen counter. It was polite, full of apology, but the message was clear—he wanted her to move out. She could leave the key under the large flat rock in the front flower garden. "P.S.," the note said. "Take a day or two if you need to make arrangements."

Marybeth straightened the guest room. She made the bed, carefully fluffing the pillows, tightly tucking the sheets into the box spring. She packed her two bags and sat down to write Marco's brother a thank-you note for letting her stay there the last three weeks.

Outside she waited for the taxicab, making certain to leave the key in the flower garden. A lizard scooted out when she picked up the flat wet stone. She watched it slither away, then stuck the key in the ground.

The taxi was late, and while she was waiting she decided that she would go to the airport. She could fly to Maine and stay with her older brother and his wife. Maine, a long way from Miami, was a good place to be while she thought about her next move. She could charge the airline ticket to her American Express account—she and Doug still shared an account. Doug would get the bill, and though she planned to mail him the money to cover the flight, the bill would be a way of letting him know where she was. Marybeth called her brother from a noisy pay phone at the airport. They couldn't hear each other that well, but she told him she and Doug were having problems and that she needed a place to stay. "By all means," her brother shouted. "We'd be thrilled to have you. Stay as long as you like." Marybeth felt much better after her conversation with her brother—her mood was almost festive. A one-way ticket to Boston with connections to Portland in hand, she went into the small, smoky bar near her gate and ordered a beer. This was the happiest she had been in days. The bartender refused to charge her for the drink. "It's on the house," he insisted.

Marybeth left some money under her empty glass, but the bartender gave it back.

"What I really want is your phone number," he said. He had large gray eyes. His hair was combed away from his forehead and held in place with a generous amount of styling gel.

That money was the only cash Marybeth had. She told him she was a tourist, without any real plans to be back this way. She waved good-bye and hurried over to the gate where the attendants had already made several announcements, urging the Boston-bound passengers to board the aircraft.

Marco had become friendly with the woman who slept in the lounge chair while her kids played in the pool. She was a single mother—a nonworking woman who collected large child support checks from her ex-husband. Marco was surprised to find out that she didn't live in the condominium complex—she certainly used the pool more than any of the other tenants. She rented a bungalow down the street that didn't have a front yard, much less a pool. Marco had asked her out a couple of times, and she laughed as if she found this proposal hysterical. He didn't know what this was supposed to mean, so he was silent and watched her laugh. Finally she told him that she was giggling because she smoked a joint every morning before coming down to the pool.

"What about your kids?" he asked. "What if they run into some trouble in the water?"

"I can't swim," she told him. "Stoned or not, I wouldn't be able to help them."

"But you're their mother." Marco found her attitude extremely casual—and he was no longer sure he wanted to date her.

"Being a mother doesn't make me less terrified of the water," she told him. She crossed her legs Indian-style and used the side of her thumbnail to rub the berry stains off the back of her thighs. It was a provocative move, and Marco was attracted to her all over again.

"Besides," the woman told him. "Look at them. They're great swimmers."

The kids were good swimmers. Still, Marco didn't think it was a good idea to let them swim without supervision. He became a self-appointed lifeguard and kept a hawk's gaze on the kids when they were in the pool. He made them take half-hour time-outs where they would lie on their towels or on their multicolored floating raft.

It was during one of these time-outs when the police came by the condominium to put up the evacuation notices. Marco was at the soda machine trying to buy Cokes for everybody when the police car pulled into the parking lot. The red and blue lights were flashing, but there was no siren. Marco put some coins in the slot and selected the Coke button. Nothing moved. He tried the other buttons, but nothing came out, not even his quarters when he pushed the change return. A policeman called him over, and Marco walked gingerly across the pavement. There was no shade and the heat scorched his bare feet.

"We're evacuating for Andrew." The policeman cupped his hands over his mouth as if he was speaking through a megaphone. Marco was confused. Marco thought the cop was talking about the scandal with Prince Andrew and his wife. The duchess had recently been photographed topless with her new American male friend, and the scandal was splashed on the cover of every magazine and newspaper.

"Hurricane Andrew," the policeman told him. "They named the tropical depression two days ago." He spoke of the storm as if he were already familiar with it—as if he already knew what kind of damage it was going to do. The sky was a light gray color, it looked like it might rain, but a destructive storm didn't seem possible.

"No heroics," the policeman told Marco. "No macho stuff like trying to stay through the storm. It's going to be the big one, and we don't want to have to come through here picking up the bodies. If we find you here after midnight, we'll arrest you."

Marco, suddenly full of purpose, went back to the pool, eager to explain the situation to the woman. But she and the kids were gone. He called her name and listened to the echo of his voice as it bounced off the high-rise. They had vanished, taking with them every one of their neon-colored floating devices.

The National Guard moved into Miami immediately after the storm. The majority of the troops were sent south of the city to neighborhoods hit the hardest. But others lined the streets in Coconut Grove, Key Biscayne, and parts of Coral Gables. They stood on every corner, dressed in camouflage uniforms, with guns slung over their shoulders. Hired to protect people's property from looters, they were also helpful carrying cartons of water from cars to kitchens or dragging tree branches off front lawns. The water pipes in Doug's condominium complex burst, and the building kept the storm evacuation. There was no word on when the tenants would be able to move back in, but rumor had it that the owners were not going to repair the building. It would be cheaper for them to cut their losses and simply abandon the place.

Despite the hassle crossing the Rickenbacker Causeway—the guards there had been ordered not to let anyone but residents with a current Florida driver's license listing a Key Biscayne address across—Doug went out almost every evening after the storm. His apartment was ruined. Water had damaged almost all of his possessions, staining everything and leaving behind a strong mildewy odor. Still, it was interesting to come and survey things. He liked being out there with the other tenants. He liked talking about the storm with them. Doug got friendly with the National Guardsman who stood just inside the driveway near the white stone griffins at the entrance to the condominium complex. The guard was bored—there was very little protecting to do—and he told Doug that for a couple of extra bucks he'd be glad to help Doug move some of the heavy stuff out of the apartment.

Marybeth was happy in Maine with her brother and his wife. Her brother had a small house in a resort town right on the ocean. The water was too cold to swim in, and most of the people who went there for the summer were older and did not sit out in the sun, but the feeling around the place was that of a beach town. Vacationing was high on everybody's list of things to do. Everyone had to have fun. No one watched television. No one read the newspapers. No one spoke of things they had to do. Her brother and his wife were big-time Boston lawyers. This month at the ocean was their only vacation, and they were aggressive about having a blast. There were parties, clambakes, cocktail hours every night, and although she was apprehensive about being an intruder, Marybeth was swept into the good-time atmosphere.

"This is what family is for," her brother told her.

"Thank you," Marybeth said. Her brother must have said something to his friends about Marybeth's situation. People were continually approaching her and giving her their views on marriage. The women were continually giving her their opinions of men.

"Pigs. Snakes. Clowns. A waste of time."

Marybeth would sip her too spicy, too strong Bloody Marys and nod in agreement as people told her about their first divorces. No one asked about Doug. No one asked her to explain her situation. No one asked her what she planned to do next. She drank wine in the afternoon with her sister-in-law and helped out in the kitchen making cheese dips, saying nothing about what she had left behind in Miami.

After Andrew, the city of Miami became an overnight news sensation. People wanted to see other people suffering. Marco got busy right away. His expired press pass in hand, he was out taking photographs the morning after the storm. No one turned him away. With their homes turned inside out, they didn't seem to mind the fishbowl quality their lives had taken on. People let Marco take any kind of photograph. They would do anything he wanted.

He was getting paid by the *Herald*. No one had told him he was rehired, but the first day he went in with his photographs, the special features editor told him they were great. He splashed them across the front page the next morning. He told Marco he'd take a look at anything Marco had. His old co-workers acted like he had never been laid off. The only difference seemed to be that he didn't have a desk and found no reason to stick around, so he didn't.

He was in Homestead, an area the locals had nicknamed Tent City, when a woman approached him and asked if he had access to a darkroom.

"I'm with the *Herald*," Marco said proudly.

"Damn," the woman said. "I'm in desperate need of a dark-room."

Tent City was the place to be for hurricane photographs. It was here where they had the long water lines, where people sat on what used to be their front lawns watching people watch them. It was here that Governor Clinton, making a solid run for the presidency, landed his helicopter. Marco shot a whole roll of him hugging people. Clinton was a great subject—he'd hug anybody.

The woman held up a brown shopping bag and rattled it in Marco's face. Marco looked at her curiously.

"It's full of film that I'd like to get developed," she said. "I'm working freelance, and this stuff should have gone to the majors three days ago."

Marco did not tell her that three days ago nothing was happening in Miami except the heat. Three days ago, the ma-jors—she was talking about the big magazines: *Time, Newsweek, People*—were not interested in the city of Homestead, Florida. Instead he took her to the apartment where he had been staying. He had run into the mother of a high school friend the morning after Andrew, and when he told her that he was photographing the aftermath of the storm, she offered him her garage apartment right across from the Coral Gables Golf Course, rent free.

Marco let the woman develop all twenty-seven rolls in the tiny, windowless bathroom. When she was finished he took her to the post office and she express mailed fourteen pounds of hurricane photographs off to magazine editors across the country. She offered to buy him dinner, and Marco accepted.

"I'm on my way to Hawaii," the woman told Marco. "There's a ninety-five percent chance that a tidal wave is going to blow right across the big island."

Marco was disappointed that she'd be leaving Miami so soon. She was not a beautiful woman, but she had great hair, and Marco liked the way she talked—full of speed and energy, as if she was late for something really important.

"Of course after this storm, it'll be second fiddle, but I can probably make some cash."

They were on the beach, at a fabulously expensive restaurant. Marco chewed his pâté slowly. He wanted the meal to last. He sipped some wine. The busboy put two more pats of butter on the overflowing butter dish.

"But where I'd really like to go is Colombia," she said and smiled at Marco. "Do you have any interest in going to Colombia?"

"Colombia?"

"Drug wars make great photo opportunities," the woman said. "But I won't go to South America by myself. Women aren't safe there alone. Why don't you come with me?"

"How would we get there?" Marco asked. But he had already made more money in the past three days than he had the rest of the year. He could actually afford a ticket to Colombia.

"Credit-card it," the woman said. "We'll make back what we

spend going there like that." She snapped her finger and the waiter, thinking she wanted something, came to the table. When he saw that they were not finished with their meal, that the water glasses were full, that the butter dish had just been replenished, he asked the woman what she needed.

"I need for him to say yes." The woman was staring at Marco.

The waiter must have thought it was a marriage proposal. When Marco nodded yes—yes he would go to Colombia with this woman—he had been carrying a valid passport around with him since he was a sophomore in high school and had never been out of the country, it was time to leave Miami, it was time to do something—the waiter offered them his congratulations and best wishes.

Doug's accounting firm got progressively busier after the hurricane hit. The first week was quiet as people assessed their problems. The next week they were swamped. Everyone in Miami was having money problems—financial situations, as the firm called them—and the whole city needed accountants. Doug went to the airport one afternoon to pick up a client who was coming in from Washington, D.C. The man was an important, busy client, and Doug's firm thought it was a good idea to meet people like this as soon as they landed. Discussion of the problems got under way immediately, and by the time clients got to the office, they would be ready to sign the appropriate form. A time-saving method, yet one that didn't make clients feel they were being cheated.

Doug thought the man was coming in on the 12:20 from Dulles, but when he called his secretary to confirm, she told him the client had missed that flight and would be on the next one. It was scheduled to arrive at two o'clock. With not enough time to go back to the office, Doug went to have lunch. The nearby bars and restaurants were filled, so he walked all the way to C terminal and took the elevator up to the Sheraton. The hostess seated him near the window, and he had a cup of chicken soup and watched the planes taxi out to the runways. He was exhausted. Before his club sandwich arrived, he was asleep.

He woke up a few minutes later. He lifted his eyes and saw a woman in a dark-blue uniform standing in front of him. His head was still heavy with sleep. He asked her for a cup of coffee.

She laughed and pointed to the gold wings on her lapel. She worked for an airline company. It took him a few minutes to recognize Marco's ex-girlfriend.

Doug stood up and was immediately dizzy as the blood rushed to his head. She held him steady and he began to apologize.

"Looks like living in a national disaster area has been hard on you," she teased.

"I've just been so busy," Doug apologized.

"Don't you sleep at home anymore?"

"I don't have a home anymore." Doug wanted to explain what it was like to live in a hotel room every night. He had picked a great place on the beach, a hotel that delivered room-service meals twenty-four hours a day—except most nights he was so tired he couldn't do anything but watch television and listen to the sounds of people partying in the beachfront cafes.

Marco's ex-girlfriend sat down and ate both halves of his club sandwich. She asked after Marco, and Doug told her that he hardly ever saw him anymore. He was busy with storm photographs.

She was flying the Miami–Pittsburgh route about three times a month. It put her in Miami for a few days at a time. She had tickets to the relief concert that night on Miami Beach—Phil Collins, Sting, and Gloria Esteban—proceeds would go to help the people whose lives had been devastated by the storm.

"Do you have any interest in going?" she asked. "It doesn't start until eight. Maybe that's too late for you?"

Doug smiled. He had always liked Marco's ex-girlfriend. She was smart, witty, and very, very sarcastic.

Marybeth's brother introduced her to a man who lived in the re-sort town all year. He was an ornithologist who made his money working for the Audubon Society collecting and recording data of rare or strange sightings. He was the one people called when they saw a pack of bald eagles or a white-tailed hawk south of the Mason-Dixon line. He recorded it and, if he judged it worthy, would send it to the national headquarters, where it would get published in the quarterly report of the Audubon Society. He was very interested in Marybeth and asked her about the bird population down south.

"Pelicans," Marybeth said. "Seagulls."

"I imagined you'd have a lot more color," he told her. "Birds reflect their environment, you know."

They were walking on the beach. The day was warm, but the water was still ice-cold, so they stayed up away from the tides. The parties were winding down, and Marybeth was beginning to worry about what would happen after Labor Day.

"Have you ever heard about people having webbed feet?" Marybeth suddenly turned to her neighbor. He was a small man. She could feel him looking at her all the time, and she found that she didn't mind his intense gaze.

"It's a sign of superior intelligence," he told her, and she stared at him inquisitively to see if he was joking. As always, he seemed to be perfectly serious.

"Why?" he said. "Do you know someone who has webbed appendages?"

Marybeth was wearing tennis shoes, and she wiggled her toes and felt the wet rubber sole. "I used to," she said, and took the man's hand. She found him strange but attentive. He was the only single man in the small resort town, and she liked the fact that he liked her.

Doug hadn't been to his old condominium in several weeks. Most of his things were moved out—he still had boxes in the storage area, but nothing he needed. He drove out one afternoon—the guard at the causeway tollbooth waved him through with barely a glance. There had been some building on Key Biscayne, but most of the island was quiet—the nightclubs and hotels had all closed down. Doug was surprised to see the same National Guardsman standing outside his complex. He was asleep—his head thrown back against the illuminated stone griffin—snoring loudly. Doug called out "Hey" at least five times before waking him.

"Sorry," the guy said and stood slowly.

"Kind of dull out here?" Doug asked. The palm trees that had been knocked down during the storm had not been removed. Light-green foliage covered their long trunks like moss.

"Deadly," the guy said. "I don't know why they bother with this post. Nothing happens. Nothing's going to happen."

"Yeah," Doug agreed, though he did not believe this. He looked to the ocean. Something silvery was washing in with the tide. It looked like it might be a manatee, and he kept watching as it moved closer to the shoreline. The turbulent waters had scared most of the marine life away, and fishermen were complaining that almost everything had moved into calmer areas north of Miami. Everything, that is, except the manatees, who clung to the seawall.

What rolled onto the beach was a garbage can. A silver alley can that had probably been floating in the bay since the day of the storm.

"I feel like I'm going to be standing here staring into space for the rest of my life," the guy said and then groaned, as if this thought caused him great pain.

Doug did not agree with this at all. "Just wait," he warned the guy. "Just you wait and see." The last year had made him a firm believer in change. Given some time and enough destruction, Doug knew that almost anything could happen.

We're in Meadville

HICH MEANS THAT WE ARE forty miles south of Erie, Pennsylvania, one hundred miles east of Cleveland, Ohio, and only about sixty feet from the bar where we are going to find Claire a new boyfriend. A minute ago Pete was driving us there, but now he and Evan are pushing a station wagon into the gas station. The owner of the car is the woman who runs the American Red Cross Society in Meadville. She knew she was low on gas, but tried to make it to the Boron station, the only place open on a Sunday here in this town of 20,000.

Claire sits quietly in the front seat watching them struggle up the incline that rises just before the gas pumps.

"Wouldn't it be easier if they just brought a gallon of gasoline to the car?" I ask. The heat vents blow out stale air and I sit back to avoid the draft.

"The guy who runs the station won't keep gas cans," Claire says. "He's afraid people would steal them." Claire knows most everything about everybody in Meadville.

"That's a pretty big car," I say, though I'm really thinking that it's a stupid thing to run out of gas.

Claire turns around to face me. "Did Pete tell you he was going to break up with me?"

I shake my head.

"Did he say anything to Evan?"

"Not that I know of."

"Would Evan tell you that kind of thing?" Claire is wearing makeup, the works—light brown eye shadow and rose lip liner. I want to tell her that she looks pretty, because she does. But she would think I was just having a pity party for her and would tell me it's not right to feel sorry for her.

"I don't know," I say. Evan and I have only been dating for two months, and there's a lot I don't know about him.

"I mean, does he usually tell you things that Pete tells him?" Claire has a slight overbite—as if she has too many teeth in her mouth—which makes her whistle certain words. Sometimes I find myself imitating her.

But just at that minute, I can't think of what Evan and I talk about. Mostly we do things to keep ourselves busy. We go for long drives into the Pennsylvania countryside and buy things at the Amish markets we don't need and will never use. We drive fifty minutes to play pool at a roadside bar and eat microwaved chicken wings and cheddar cheese french fries cooked in vinegar. We spend time in Erie, in Cleveland, in Pittsburgh, so we can remember that we are not from this small town, but are only working here. We try to convince ourselves that the teaching jobs we have at this small Methodist college are only temporary.

We tell ourselves that we will not be doing this forever and we try to ignore the fact that we are beginning to act small-town.

But it's true. We are starting to act like the people in Meadville. Why else would I get so excited when I see yard sale signs? Why else would Evan go on a weeklong fishing trip with some locals when he's never fed a line before? And why else would Pete agree that it was his duty to find Claire a new boyfriend if he was going to break up with her? Why would someone not influenced by this small-town life promise he'd spend a whole day looking for his replacement? Pete says it's like some sort of drug got into his system, clouding his better judgment and making him do all kinds of things he wouldn't normally do.

Claire is from Meadville. I watch her as she looks out at the streets. Gray and dull, it has been raining since the start of the weekend. I try to imagine what Claire sees as she stares at this place that she has always called her home. Her family was old oil money—some of the original settlers who first discovered the stuff. They still live in the mansion on the hill overlooking the now-closed railroad station. At one time it must have reflected the opulence of this boomtown, but any glory has long ago faded. There is not even a memory of it.

"I wish he had told me sooner," Claire complains. "It's almost summer. I don't want to spend the summer without a boyfriend."

I agree with her, though I do not quite understand the significance of seasonal dating. Pete told me he's not really sure why he's breaking up with Claire. It has to do with everything, but mostly it has to do with the fact that he no longer enjoys spending time with her. And judging by the way she's acting right now—bossy and bitchy—I can see why he's not happy with their relationship.

"We better find someone today," Claire says. "I mean it."

And she does mean it. That's why we've agreed to spend the afternoon searching. She wants us all to give 100 percent in this search. Meadville's not that big a town, but there is a high concentration of bars. Or, as Claire calls them, places where potential prospects are at large.

Evan and Pete return, and the car instantly smells of their wet clothes and their perspiration. Evan gets in the backseat and apologizes as he brushes up next to me. I tell him I don't mind. There's something relaxing about our relationship. We don't have much to fight about—there's nothing to get stressed out about in Meadville. We have told each other that we love each other, but I think it's a given that we would not be going out together if the choice of mates were multiplied.

Pete starts the car. "Now we're ready," he says. "Where to?" He asks as if we have not spent two hours at the diner deciding on the order of bars we'd be frequenting. Claire has them listed on a napkin.

"I told you," Claire snaps. "We're going to Otter's first."

"That's right. On to Otter's." Pete toots the horn. A man on the street corner stares.

I see that Pete is struggling to start the day on a festive note, so I slide forward into the stale drafts of air and join the conversation.

"Which one is Otter's?" I ask Claire. The bar is only a block away, but I want to get the conversation rolling.

"It's got a pool table. The jukebox is in the back," Claire explains.

"It's on North Street," Evan says. He is watching the rain with what seems to be determined concentration and I don't bother to tell him that there are over fifteen bars on North Street and they all have pool tables and jukeboxes in the back.

"We were there in February," Pete looks in the rearview mirror to talk to me. "The night when the undergrads came in and one of them threw up on the dance floor."

The bar comes to mind instantly—orange lounge chairs that look like they belong in a Florida motel lobby, not a wood-paneled bar in northern Pennsylvania. The student was one of my freshman composition students. I thought it might be awkward the next time I saw her in class, but she came in on Monday bright-eyed and cheerful. I don't think she remembered, or maybe she never even knew, that I was the one who drove her home and put her to bed that night.

Pete pulls into the parking lot and we get out of the car. The rain is lighter, but still falling. The potholes are filling with water. I walk around a puddle. Pete doesn't see it and steps right in it. He curses. His pant legs are already soaked from pushing the car into the gas station. It doesn't make much of a difference. I don't feel like drinking so early, but bar coffee is unheard of in Meadville.

We follow Claire into the bar, but before she gets all the way in she turns around and walks back out. The four of us collide in the doorway.

"Where're you going?" Pete stops her. "What's wrong?"

"There's no one here," Claire announces. "I'm not wasting my time in a bar without men."

The bartender is on the customer side of the bar eating a bag of potato chips. She seems unconcerned as to whether or not we stay.

Claire reads her napkin when we get back into the car. "The Sports Page." She announces the next bar.

"I don't know that one," Pete says.

"Yes you do," she tells him. Her makeup is still fresh, but her face is hardening with frustration. Perhaps she is already getting anxious about the time we are losing, the time we are wasting.

"Remind me again," Pete says.

"Downtown. Right next to the tanning place."

Pete still hesitates, but heads south, which is in the general direction of the library and the town hall. I know why he is confused. For a town the size of Meadville there are too many tanning places. There are just as many tanning places as there are restaurants that serve dinner after six o'clock in the evening. Evan thinks they are a cover for something, I don't know what. Claire insists that the college kids use them, but there are only 1,200 students at our college and I can't believe all of them tan. There just isn't that kind of social pressure to look good up here.

From the outside, the Sports Page looks identical to Otter's. The parking lot is full of potholes filling with water and the same OPEN sign hangs in the window to the right of the door. Only this time, Claire informs us that this place looks like it's going to be good.

"This is what I need," she says pointing to the half-dozen cars in the parking lot. "There's some action here."

Most of the people huddled around the bar are men. This is a good thing, it means we can stay. The guys are watching the TV, which is tuned to a beer commercial inside a bar. It looks an awful lot like the one we're in, which makes perfect sense to me.

"Don't act like you're with me," Claire tells us. "I don't want these guys to think I'm part of a couple."

We start to walk to one of the back tables, but stop as Claire continues talking.

"Because I'm not," she says. "Am I?"

"You're not what?" I ask. I don't always understand what she's talking about and have gotten used to asking her to repeat or explain herself.

"Not part of a couple anymore," Claire says. "Am I, Pete?"

Someone has glued pennies to the wall. When I first saw it, I thought it was just that—pennies stuck on the wall—but Pete told me it's supposed to be a baseball diamond. The spray-painted pennies—the rows of yellow, red, and blue—are the fans sitting in the stands. I still can't see it, but I'm probably looking at it from the wrong angle.

"Am I part of a couple anymore, Pete?" She's staring at him.

"No," Pete tells her, and then he tells Evan and me that he'll be right back.

"I was just checking," Claire announces. "Just checking to see if you had changed your mind. You know, you might have slept on your decision and reconsidered. It's no fun being alone in the summer in Meadville."

"I haven't changed my mind, Claire," Pete tells her and then leaves the bar.

"Where's he going?" I ask Evan, who only shrugs and looks away. Evan has been unusually quiet the past couple of days. I don't know him well enough to know if these are his regular mood swings or if he's suffering from spring cabin fever. He's not pouting, but you can tell he's not fired up about the day's entertainment. Maybe he thinks the whole thing is stupid or just too small-town. Maybe he is bored. I hope he will tell me if something is wrong, that he will talk to me when he has something to say.

Claire bellies up to the bar next to a man who offers to buy her a drink. Claire raises the glass to thank him, then sips the drink in short swallows.

"Do you want something?" I ask Evan. I reach in my back

pocket for my money. I used to carry a purse before I started living in Meadville, but now there is no need for anything except cash. No bar takes credit cards or checks, and makeup, even lipstick, seems unnecessary.

When Pete comes back in, he walks the long way around the pool table so as not to bother Claire. The bartender brings us a round of Rolling Rock longnecks. It's brewed in central Pennsylvania, and every bar in the state keeps a full stock of it.

"What's the score?" Pete asks after we have paid for the beer. I think he is talking about the basketball game. I tell him I haven't been watching and he says he's talking about Claire. "Has she found someone new? Can we go home now?" He smiles and I can tell he's being sarcastic.

"That guy bought her a drink," I say. I don't want Pete's replacement to be that easy to find. I do not want to go home right away. I rent an apartment half a mile from the college. It's the whole second floor of a large Victorian home. I pay three hundred dollars, including utilities. It would be a steal anywhere else. I don't even tell my out-of-state friends how much I pay because they wouldn't believe it, but I can't explain to them how depressing it gets. Especially on Sundays when my downstairs neighbor has her in-laws over for an early afternoon meal. The husband/son is always late and the wife and his parents fight about whose fault it is that he isn't there. "If you hadn't done this—if you hadn't done that—if you—if you—if you—if you." It goes on until the son/husband comes tearing down the street on his motorcycle. Within minutes, everyone's laughing and eating and having a good time and I'm upstairs in my apartment surrounded by the echoes of their fight.

Pete gets up and puts some quarters in the jukebox. Evan continues to stare out into space and I'm suddenly irritated at his silence.

"You okay?" I ask him.

He nods, suddenly intent on wiping the condensation off his bottle. He wipes the dampness on the cocktail napkin and drinks without saying anything.

"You seem quiet," I say. It's true, and hardly worth saying. But I start to wonder if he is mad at me for something. We went out on Friday night. Everything seemed fine. We went to the Chestnut Street Bar for dinner, drove to the other side of town to see what movie was showing. It was *Indiana Jones and the Temple of Doom*, which was playing a week ago, so we went to Pete's instead and had a few beers with him and Claire. Afterward we went to my apartment and watched the Lakers on cable. Evan doesn't sleep in past eight o'clock, even on weekends, so the next morning he got up and made coffee and left before I woke up. We didn't have sex that night. Neither one of us made a move. But we don't always have sex every time we go out. The relationship is a bit low-key, but I think it's because there's nothing to do in Meadville. We sometimes get bored with each other, but all couples go through that, even in cities where there are plenty of restaurants, and movies that change more than once a month. In places where there are interesting sights, interesting people.

"Okay, folks," Claire is at our table clapping her hands like a football coach. She has already buttoned her coat. "Let's go."

"What's wrong with that guy?" Pete asks.

"Which guy?" Claire shakes her hair loose from her coat collar.

"The one who bought you the drink."

"Ugly."

"You think he's ugly? I don't think he's ugly at all," Pete tries to stall. It's still raining. I can hear the drops falling on the roof. I don't feel like leaving either, but it's obvious that Pete's not going to win this fight.

"Real ugly," Claire says.

"You're not getting picky on us, are you?" Pete asks.

"I'm not getting anything except out of this bar," Claire says. Evan stands and she locks her arm in his. "You know what I really want?" She is talking to Evan, not to Pete or me. Evan tells her he can't imagine.

"I really want to find someone as cute as you," she says.

I am surprised by this comment. I have never heard her pay anyone a compliment, not even Pete when they first started going out. Evan has his back to me so I can't see how he's taking the compliment.

We only drink one beer at the third bar. The guys there are people Claire know from Meadville High School and she tells us that they're all married. Pete points out that there might be one or two who are divorced by now. It's been ten years since her graduation. Claire shakes her head. "People get married in this town and they stay married. There's no reason to get divorced. Everyone's got the same problems. Not enough money, too much drinking, and too many kids. Those kinds of things don't change when you get a divorce."

"What about death? Do you think maybe you could find a widower?" Pete asks her. "Doesn't anybody die in this town?"

"Not before they're supposed to." Claire is not in the mood for his humor, but I laugh at the joke. Claire hisses at me.

In the fourth bar Pete and I start up a game of pool. Evan and Claire are sitting next to each other, and before I even get a turn, Claire is ready to go. She puts her fingers in her mouth and blows a sharp whistle in our direction.

"Let's go," she orders and holds the door open. The bartender yells at her, asking her if she grew up in a barn or what. Claire ignores him and glares at Pete and me.

"This is the longest scavenger hunt in the world," Pete says. He puts his pool cue back on the rack.

I try a shot, but just then Claire whistles again and I don't even make contact with the cue ball. My bladder is full of beer, but there is no time for a bathroom stop.

Evan and Claire are already in the backseat by the time Pete and I get to the car. They are not talking, but I somehow feel that we have taken sides, that Evan is siding with Claire against Pete and me, even though I do not understand what we're fighting about.

Claire calls out the next bar and then goes back to whispering with Evan.

"Who said anything about going to Hunter's?" Pete says. "We never agreed on Hunter's."

"It's on the list," Claire says. "Right here on the list." She tosses the napkin into the front seat. It lands between Pete and me, but neither of us touches it.

"Couldn't we go somewhere closer to town?" Pete asks.

"The guys in there just told me that it's turkey day out there," Claire says. "That always attracts a crowd. Guys go for that kind of thing."

"I don't want to get into that mess," Pete says. "Isn't there another place we could try?" It's obvious that Pete has lost his energy for Claire's boyfriend search. I understand why. Hunter's is seventeen miles east of Meadville in a place called Frenchtown. The "town" part of the name is an exaggeration. There isn't any town out there, just a few deserted houses. The bar is popular enough. Set right between Meadville and Titusville, it's got a reputation for the best barbecue wings in northwestern Pennsylvania.

Turkey competitions are common in this part of the country.

At least that's what people tell me. It's a spring competition for the best turkey. Before I went to one, I thought the turkeys would be alive. I imagined the bar crowded with farmers modeling their turkeys the way dog owners show their dogs. I didn't think there'd be tricks or anything. I mean I didn't think the turkeys would lie down or beg or shake anybody's hand, but it did surprise me when I went to one and saw that the turkeys are all dead. And they're huge. Most of them weigh more than dogs—up to and over one hundred pounds. The turkeys are judged mainly for size—biggest is best—but the judges also score and remark on the color and overall feel of the turkey, how much white and dark meat it will yield.

Pete drives northeast, totally the opposite way from Hunter's, and Claire keeps quiet. I turn to look at her a few times to see if she is fuming. Both she and Evan are staring out the window. They're looking out the same window—out across the marsh where two hawks are diving into the tall grasses. Pete stops the car, then makes a 180-degree turn right in the middle of the road. Claire sighs to let him know that she's acknowledging his giving in.

The parking lot of Hunter's is not just full—it's packed. Cars and pickup trucks are double-parked along the side of the one-story red building. The cars are up on the grass and all along the shoulder of the highway. Pete circles twice, but no one's leaving. He goes back the same way we drove in and pulls up behind the long line of cars on the side of the road. Hunter's is a long way ahead.

"You having fun?" I ask Evan after we are both out of the car. I try walking next to him, but it's difficult with the potholes, the weeds, and the cars driving by at sixty miles an hour.

"What do you think?" Evan asks. His attitude disappoints me because it's not such a bad afternoon. Looking for Claire's boy-

friend has given the afternoon shape. It's not just listless movement from one place to the other, like how we usually spend the
weekends when there's nothing to distract us from the long afternoons and the even longer nights.

"It's not that bad, is it?" I say. He is walking fast and I have to
half skip, half run to keep up with him.

"It's not a whole lot of fun," he says, and this time I can't
ignore the tone of his voice. He's not happy, and his foul mood
is directed at me. As if the day is my fault.

"What is it?" I ask. "What's so wrong with everything?"

His eyebrows are pulled together and he looks exhausted, as
if the three or four beers we've drunk have sapped all his energy.
He really seems to be struggling to make it through this day.

Behind us I hear Claire and Pete—their footfalls on the gravel.
"Hey, slow down, you two," Pete calls out. "There's no race to
get there. Hunter's isn't going anyplace soon."

Claire catches up to us and starts walking alongside Evan and
me, forcing me onto the blacktop. I drop back and let her go on
ahead with Evan. Pete seems happier than he was in the car and
we start talking about summer vacation. Pete has been teaching
in Meadville longer than I have. He's the one who told me you
have to plan your vacations way in advance so that you have
something to look forward to. He told me that it makes the days
more tolerable if you know exactly when you'll be leaving.

The sound of a gun being fired comes out of nowhere. I stop
in surprise and spin around to see where it's coming from. It
sounds farther away than it really is because of all the open space,
but the man who shot the gun is standing in the field right across
from the bar. Evan yells for us to watch out. He grabs Claire by
the shoulders and pulls her to the ground with him. The two
of them roll between the cars and take cover under the back
bumper of a rusted-out LeMans.

"It's okay, guys," Pete says. "He's not aiming at us."

I can see the man perfectly. He looks like a hunter. He's wearing a plaid overcoat and a red cap. He's got the rifle balanced on his shoulder and fires a second shot at the turkey standing a couple of yards in front of him.

Evan and Claire stay huddled under the bumper. They must think they're still in some kind of danger. "It's just some guy killing his turkey," I tell them. "It's nothing to worry about."

"Look," Pete points to the field near the group of abandoned trailers. "He's right over there."

Pete and I both laugh when the two of them stand up. Evan has rolled them through the mud and their clothes are streaked with the damp dirt. Claire has it worse than Evan. Her coat must have been open and her sweater is muddy.

"You really think someone was out to get you?" Pete asks Evan. "You must really be a city boy."

"Hey, the guy had a gun," Evan says. He tries to brush the dirt off the front of his jacket, but his hands are covered in mud and he only streaks it worse.

They look so odd standing there all dirty and I can't stop laughing. Pete reaches in his pocket and hands Claire the crumpled bar napkin he must have picked up off the front seat. Instead of wiping the dirt from her face, she blows her nose. Evan tells me that he doesn't see what's so funny.

"You would if you could see the two of you," I say.

Claire must have rolled through a puddle, because the ends of her hair are wet. She brushes them with her fingers so they won't tangle.

Evan spits out the dirt in his mouth. "I'm going to go wash up," he says. "You want to go on ahead with me?"

Claire says yes and the two of them walk toward Hunter's. Pete and I watch them leave.

"I guess I shouldn't have laughed at him," I say. I'm sorry that I've made Evan mad.

"It's no big deal," Pete says. He is still trying to keep the afternoon light, full of fun. "He'll get over it."

"You think so?" The clouds shift a bit and rain falls for a second as if the clouds are shaking the drops loose. It is not that cold out, but I'm chilled and would like to go inside where it will be dry. We go on walking.

A small group is watching the guy kill his turkey. We can hear them taunting him when we approach.

"You're supposed to kill the turkey at home, guy." I recognize the men in the group. I don't know any of them by name, but I have seen them around town at the grocery store, in the bars. We must look familiar to them too, because one of them waves. We stop and stare. The man clears the rifle and then goes over to his turkey.

The men head for Hunter's. We follow a few feet behind.

"I don't know why he does that," we overhear them saying. "Every year he waits to kill his bird until he gets here."

"That's 'cause he falls in love with it."

"It's got to be something like that." Their voices echo over the open fields. The guy with the turkey is right behind us. He can hear what they're saying about him.

"Is that what it is?" one of them shouts. "Are you in love with your bird?"

"Just forgot to kill her," the guys says in his own defense. "I just forgot to do it until right now."

This cracks everyone up, including Pete and me.

Hunter's is full. Most everyone is standing around the dance floor with their turkeys. There are plenty of empty tables on one side of the bar. I tell Pete I have to go to the bathroom. I've had to go since we left the last bar. He says he'll get us a table.

Claire is waiting for me when I walk out of the stall. She has washed the dirt off her face, but her sweater is stained with large brown-green circles. Her elbow is cut but clean and she has matching dirt circles on the knees of her pants. She is talking, but with the sound of the toilet flushing, I don't hear what she's saying.

"Listen," she says and points her finger at me. "I want to talk to you about the way you treat Evan," she says. Her makeup has faded, making her look younger. Her sentences are clear, her words not slurred, though it takes me several minutes to understand what it is that she wants. "You don't treat him very good. Not very good at all."

"I don't?" I am surprised by her accusation, but do not deny it.

"Not at all," she moves closer. I am trapped in the corner, where the smell of industrial cleaning solution is strong. "He's a real sweetheart. He is always saying nice things and you don't care about him."

"I think you're being melodramatic, Claire." I try to step away from her, but she puts her arms on either side of my shoulders, caging me in further. Guys have been buying her drinks all afternoon, and I imagine she's a bit out of it.

"You better start appreciating him a whole lot more than you do."

"I appreciate him just fine." I push away her arms to break free of her trap.

Our conversation is so strange, even for Claire, that I don't take her seriously until I go out to the table and find Pete sitting there alone.

I assume Evan is in the bathroom. The dance floor is packed with people and turkeys. The women hold them like babies, cradled in their arms, while the men hold them by their necks, their bodies dragging on the wood floor. The bar smells of the dead birds. It's a rotting smell, nothing at all like Thanksgiving.

"Evan left," Pete tells me.

"He left?" I ask. I give the bar a quick search as if I don't believe him. "Why? Why'd he leave?"

"He said he was tired," Pete tells me. "He wasn't in the mood for all this."

"How's he going to get home?" I didn't think Pete would lend his truck to Evan. Not that they're not buddies, but Pete wouldn't leave us stranded out in Frenchtown. It's not like we could call a cab or hop on a bus.

"Randy Coyne didn't make it into the final competition," Pete says, "He was eliminated in round two. Evan drove back with him." I can tell Pete is uncomfortable having this conversation. He's someone involved in something he didn't want to be. Pete stays out of other people's business.

"Randy Coyne?" I ask, and though Pete nods, I ask again. "Evan drove back to town with Randy Coyne?" It's odd that Evan would leave like that, even for the kind of dark mood he was in. He has never done something like this and I find it odder still that he would choose to ride home with Randy Coyne, who is one of the most famous locals around. Everyone can tell stories about him, even those of us who don't participate in gossip and don't listen for it. We all know that he has been blamed for every accident in town, even the burning of the Meadville Press office when there were four witnesses who swear that he was out at camp deer hunting. They did convict him of one robbery. He robbed the town bakery on its last day of business, three hours before it closed for good. The owner said that Randy didn't even have a gun. He simply asked for the money—all twenty-eight dollars and fifteen cents. The guy handed it over to Randy because, he said, he didn't think there was any reason to fight. Randy spent a month or two in the Crawford County jail. Evan's not the kind of person to drive home with someone like that. This much I know about Evan.

"Did I do something wrong?" I know Pete can't answer these questions, but I want somebody to tell me what's going on. "I mean, was Evan upset about something?"

"I don't know," Pete shrugs, then asks if I want to play a game of pool. The tables at Hunter's are usually crowded. They get serious players out there, but today, because of the contest, because there's more money at stake in turkeys, both tables are empty.

"Is Evan mad at me?"

Pete tells me he doesn't know.

"Would he tell you if he was?" I pick up a pool stick and rub rosin on the tip. It occurs to me that I sound an awful lot like Claire, and this bothers me, but I have to find out what's wrong.

"Who knows?" Pete shrugs.

"Does he talk to you about things like this?" I ask, insisting that I get an answer.

Pete breaks and the balls scatter to the sides of the table. The seven ball rolls into the corner pocket and he shoots again. I don't look to see if he makes the shot. I don't care if he cheats.

Claire walks up to us and someone follows right on her heels. I don't recognize him. I figure she's going to introduce him to Pete. It would seem fitting to end the day by letting her new boyfriend meet her old boyfriend.

"Evan's the only decent single man left in Meadville," Claire says, and again I'm so surprised by what she's saying that I don't register her remark. For a minute, I forget that I am Evan's girlfriend, but then remember and tell her that he's not so single.

"He is as far as I'm concerned." Claire moves in closer, and right then her teeth whistle. Pete smiles at the way she's trying to be so serious about everything and still sounding like a kid's toy.

"Why do you say that?" I ask. "What did Evan tell you?" I know she knows something I don't. I look to Pete to see if he is in on it, too, but he's concentrating on his shot, trying deliberately to stay out of our argument.

"He said he was planning on breaking it off with you," she tells me loud and clear. This time there is no whistle. "He said there was nothing interesting about the two of you together."

The guy behind Claire tells us that he's going to the bar. He wants to know if we want anything. "A beer, maybe some whiskey?" he offers.

"We're leaving," Claire turns slightly as if just remembering him. "You promised to give me a ride back to town anytime I wanted it, and I'm calling it quits on this place right now."

The guy seems unconcerned if they stay or go.

"I just wanted to let you know that I'm going to Evan's tonight," Claire tells me. "I don't do things behind other people's backs. I'm not sneaky or underhanded. I told Evan I wanted to come over, and he said that was fine with him. He said he'd like that just fine."

"He said that?" I ask and I put it all together and realize that Evan's leaving was his way of breaking it off with me.

Pete is quiet, not saying anything, not acting surprised, so I know that Evan must have told him that he wanted to let things cool between us.

"That's what he said," Claire says. "I promise you. I'm not making any of it up. I'm not a cheat. He said those things and I have to go now." She looks at her watch, and I wonder if she timed herself in finding a new boyfriend. Has she set a new record? Has she at least beaten her own best time?

Pete and I are quiet on the car ride home. The road turns sharply five or six times before we see the lights of town. The clouds have lifted some and the sky is almost clear, but not quite. There are no stars. From here, Meadville looks quaint, almost inviting.

"Did he just get bored?" I ask without mentioning Evan by name. "Is that what you think happened? Did he just get bored with me?"

"Maybe," Pete says. "That kind of thing happens." Then he speaks with the wisdom of someone who has lived three years in northwestern Pennsylvania. "That kind of thing happens all the time around here."

We coast down the hill into town and Pete asks me if I'm hungry.

"Not really," I say. I am upset, but I can't quite figure out what it is that bothers me. I don't think it's Evan specifically. I will miss him, but Claire's right. We were never that good a match. I'm mad about the way he's handled the whole thing and wonder if I'll ever mention it to him or if I'll just let things go their own way.

"It's not that late," Pete tells me and I agree. Neither one of us teaches on Mondays, but we usually go into school to grade papers, to check our mail, to be around people.

"We could watch TV at my house," Pete says. "There might be a movie."

"That sounds good," I say, because it does. I would like to avoid my apartment, avoid being alone as long as possible. And just as if he has the same idea, Pete passes his house and we drive downtown. The streets are heavy with traffic. It's the high school kids cruising around the diamond, the park in the center of downtown. They circle the diamond every night in their parents' cars and trucks. If it's a nice night like it is right now, the kids from the farming community drive in and join the townies.

We drive around and around the diamond honking at one another, drinking beer, and calling out to one another. They always drive in the same direction, clockwise, as if following some predetermined pattern. Like all rituals, the customs are complicated, some not even apparent.

Pete cuts over on North Street and we get into the cruising line and follow the traffic around the gazebo, past the bronze statue of Crawford, the man who founded the county and who some say was eaten by Indians. Others insist that no one ever found his body and have no concrete proof that the Indians even touched him. We circle past the Meadville Public Library and the fifteen-foot American flag dedicated to the town by the Daughters of the American Revolution, even though there is no chapter in Meadville. We pass the funeral home where the clay point setter stands by the front door. The dog is frozen in motion. His ears stick straight up, his right paw is bent as if wounded. His face is illuminated by the small yellow spotlight. He looks almost alive. Denying all town rumors, Bradford, the owner and mortician of the funeral home, insists that it was never a real dog. He claims the statue is not his own dog killed, stuffed, and set on display. He thinks it makes the funeral home less frightening—more inviting—especially for the kids in town.

Pete turns down the radio and we lower our windows and listen to the noise and music coming from the other cars. The air is still damp from the afternoon rain. It smells of spring—of warmer days to come.

After two turns around the diamond, Pete pats the edge of the seat and asks me if I want to sit closer. I think about Evan before I make a move. Evan has made it clear that he wants out of my life. He didn't even discuss it with me. He never gave me an option or cared to hear my opinion on the matter. Our relationship doesn't seem a reason not to get close to someone else, so I do. Pete puts his arm around my shoulders. He rubs my upper arm and I cross my left hand to my chest and hold his hand so he will know I like what he is doing. We circle the diamond four more times, not saying anything important, just commenting on the trucks and the kids. Pete turns off the diamond and we drive to the west end of town where the dark streets eventually wind into Cleveland.

Pete slows the car and pulls onto the graveled shoulder in front of a farmhouse. The inside lights flicker, and the shadows bounce off the ceiling, telling us that the family is inside watching TV. They won't be paying attention to a car parked on their property. We're making out even before Pete's turned off the engine. He's holding me on the back of the neck, his grip firm on my skin, his hands warm. He pulls me into him. His kiss is strong. He seems sure that this is what he wants, and I kiss him back to tell him that I want it, too. What I'm doing no longer feels small-town. All over the world, people are called upon to replace love. It happens everywhere, even when we don't expect it. Meadville's not the exception this time. Not on this.

Me and Danno
Booking 'Em Good

OLCANOES ON UNINHABITED ISLANDS erupt without fanfare. Like a tree falling in a forest, Hawaiians ask, Is there sound if no one is there to hear it? What about fear, if no one is there to feel it? Perhaps there is only the brilliant flash of light as the fiery liquids pour down the mountainside. Maybe this is all there is.

Barney's mother warned us that the sky over our house was an odd shade of blue. My mother believed only in the Bible. She read between the lines and found good truths in these words. Superstitions were not part of her religion. She paid Barney's mother to do our wash and to iron my father's shirts, but she would not listen to her predictions of doom and despair.

Barney's mother saw dark clouds everywhere. She bowed her

head and told us to chant, "I give my heart to the sky," three times over. In this way we could be saved from the volcanic ash carried in with the evil winds.

"I give my heart to God," my mother cried. She had fallen in love with the sound of her own voice and liked to pitch it so that it rang in that sing-song way evangelists have now made an art.

"I left my heart in San Francisco," I cried.

Barney and his mother chanted their prayer, but the ash fell on our house and two weeks later my father died of a twisted liver.

The driver from the funeral home had to stop twice to wipe the ash off the windshield of the hearse. "Can't see a thing," he complained. His shirt cuffs were black with the soot that clung to everything it touched. We were an hour late to the cemetery. The funeral director and his sons were already busy with another circle of bereaved. My father and his coffin had been moved to the gazebo, where it sat in the cool shade of the coconut trees. My mother knelt on the stone steps, made the sign of the cross, and bowed her head. A few minutes later, she stood and ushered her prayer people up the paved path to the crest of the hill where they could be closer to God.

My brothers and I drank scotch from a silver flask we found in the pocket of my father's only formal dinner jacket. He probably hid it there—afraid my mother would have tossed it out with the morning trash. My mother kept a clean house. Clutter was a sign of a wandering mind; a wandering mind, the sign of a sinning body. Nothing to her had sentimental value—nothing should be saved except the soul.

My brothers only shared their stash with me because it was a special occasion. "Don't get hooked on this stuff," they warned. I was fifteen and had already been drunk more times than I could count. The hearse driver joined us in a toast to long life. To mention death in a graveyard would have been redundant.

I blacked out before the service started and don't remember burying my father. I have seen photographs of the afternoon. My blue blazer and white shirt had been pressed carefully by Barney's mother, but the expression on my face was one of impatience, as if the bus I was waiting for was late. My brother Rob, front row center, was fast asleep. Dave had wandered off by that time and was found puking in the bushes. I puked with him once we were back in the hearse. The driver shouted that we were worse than pigs. My mother said we had ruined our father's funeral. She said she did not have it in her heart to forgive us.

Barney was my best friend back then. I was not popular. He might have been my only friend. Mr. Matthews, the science teacher, once asked Barney if I had been drinking whiskey. "He reeks," the teacher said. "That's the way he always smells," Barney said. Barney was not bright. That's why he liked me.

Barney was HBC—Hawaiian-born-Chinese. His hair was black and his eyes were thick. His mother and father washed and ironed the clothes for all the families in our neighborhood, but Barney screamed in protest if you called him Chinese.

"I am western," he said. "I am from this island. I am just like you."

My parents were from a small town in northwestern Pennsylvania, where everyone complained about the good old days when there were jobs to be had. They moved to Hawaii hoping to find a financial paradise. I was born on the island of Oahu.

Not one to argue, I told Barney he was right. "We're Hawaiian-born. Natives. We'll make the tourists take pictures of us. We will ask for money, and when they won't give it to us we'll steal their expensive cameras and expose their film. Later we'll hang out in the Sheraton and Marriott parking lots and jump in front of slow-moving tourist cars. When they think we're hurt, we'll play on their fear and their pity and extort cash from the poor out-of-towners."

My father was promoted to desk manager of the Oahu Marriott after twelve years of working the midnight shift. He could say, "Here is your safety deposit box key. There is no charge for the box, but there's only one key, so if you lose or misplace it there will be a sixty dollar drilling fee," in several languages, including Japanese, Malay, Tagalog, French, German, and Spanish. He had access to the bar of the Banana-Boat-and-Moon restaurant and brought home red, white, and blue bottles of liquor, which he drank all at once.

"Let me make you a Stars-and-Stripes," he'd offer and pour the trio of liquors into a tall glass with lots of ice. It tasted like a sweet watery milk shake. I drank it as fast as I could, hoping he would give me another.

"Here's to our new country," he'd say. We'd salute each other, then break into a chorus of "The Star-Spangled Banner," "America the Beautiful," or "Michael, Row the Boat Ashore."

"The neighbors," my mother would yell from the bedroom. We shouted out cocktail invitations in loud, clear voices, but none of our neighbors ever joined our predawn patriotic celebrations.

My father was a distracted man. He liked bars and long rambling stories full of interesting characters. My brothers and I were not colorful enough for him. He wanted tough life stories. "Sagas," he'd beg for when the whiskey pinched his cheeks red. "Give me a long saga and I'll listen to every word." I bored him more than most people, and he quickly drank blenderfuls of his stars-and-stripes concoction, as if this would make me more fun.

My mother wanted daughters. She thought raising children would mean dresses with white petticoats and patent leather Mary Janes. Pink stuffed animals. Bows. She wanted to braid her daughter's hair into thick French twists and wash it with golden baby shampoo, the kind that doesn't make your eyes tear.

She thought men were wanderers. She did not trust them to be there for the long haul. She wanted daughters who would take care of her when she got old and hard of hearing.

She was never hard of hearing, but she was selective and cheap. She would pretend not to understand when people talked on the phone so that she didn't have to pay long-distance bills. In this way she avoided most conversations with her unemployed Pennsylvanian relatives, who were always looking for an invitation to the Hawaiian Islands.

She liked letters—even from her friends she saw every day. She could not spell and did not write letters herself.

She had three sons.

After the third she gave up and refused to have anything to do with our upbringing.

The way my mother tells it, she was on her way to the loony bin when she discovered God. He embraced her forcefully and fondly placed her on the right road.

We were left on our own after my father died. My mother said, "I'll sign checks for your care, but beyond that don't count on me."

She liked the church, quoting from the Bible, and raising

poodles. Poodles were amazing creatures, she insisted, though before my dad died she had not let a turtle into the house, much less a dog. Poodles, she told us over and over, did not shed. They did not need cleaning up after. She married an animal hairdresser who asked us boys to call him Captain. He was not religious, but said he respected a woman who prayed. The two of them made plans to raise poodle champions. They spent all my father's money buying poodles that won them a roomful of blue ribbons, silver-plated trophies, and shelves and shelves of ceramic poodles.

I liked beer but drank it too fast and pissed most of it away before I got a buzz. I started on Southern Comfort because that's what the G.I.s drank during World War II. The Hawaiian liquor stores had dusty shelves of the sweet-tasting liquor that no one bought. I bargained down the price, telling the shopowner I was buying it for my father.

"He's having a love affair with the bottle," I told Mr. Wang.

Mr. Wang sold me bottles at half-price until his wife discovered what I was up to. Mrs. Wang, one of my mother's disciples, knew that my father had died in November.

Mr. Wang cursed me with a horrible life because I lied on my father's grave.

I took my business elsewhere.

Tourists would always buy for me.

"Look, the native boy wants some alcohol," the just-married men would tell their wives. I was tan, dirty, and dark and wore the baggy shorts and mud-stained T-shirts of the islanders.

"How about some Jack?" I liked to stick to business. "J.B. Any of the big boys will do."

The new husbands would go into the store and the wives would stand on the street with me. I liked their pink freckled skin, the way they wrinkled their noses in the bright sunlight.

I gave the women my telephone number, which they always took but never used, though I always thought one of them might call.

I borrowed money from Barney or stole money from my mother to support my habit. My mother caught me with her wallet in my hands at least once a week. She knew I was drinking. I never lied to her about my alcohol intake.

"One daughter," she said in her prayer voice, looking at the overhead light fixture. Either God lived there, I told my brothers, or she is scared of wasp's nests.

One afternoon she was particularly whiny, and when she found me with her money in hand, she slapped me across the cheek before turning to the ceiling. "Would it have been so hard to bless me with one girl who would stay with me while my teeth fall out?" she cried.

I went into her bedroom, put on one of her muumuus, and walked around the house in her fruit-salad sandals.

The Captain thought I was funny, but he said that drunks died slow, painful deaths.

He slumped off his chair, clutching his stomach, imitating my father so closely that I wondered if Mom and the Captain hadn't been hanky-pankying before she was a widow.

My mother came in just as the Captain made it to the floor. "He swallowed a chicken bone," I said and jumped up from my chair.

She knelt in a great panic and began to give him mouth-to-mouth resuscitation.

I was lonely. Wanting to drink, but not wanting to do it alone, I went to the neighborhood bar and ordered a beer.

The nearsighted waitress served me, and I drank three bottles of beer before a customer complained that the place looked like "Romper Room."

My brothers, bored and smitten with rock fever, made plans to move to the mainland. Traitors, I called them.

"Who will take care of Mom?" I asked.

"The good Captain," they answered. "And you."

They let me come to their going-away beer bash on the beach as a consolation prize. They knew they were abandoning a sinking ship.

I was fifteen and there were girls at the party in string bikinis. I found a pack of cards and walked around asking if anyone felt like a quick game of strip poker.

I drank keg beer and told the HBC turning the spit that I wanted to eat the eyes of the pig.

He told me only rats ate the eyes of other animals.

The partygoers cheered me on. I swallowed the eyes whole, washing them down with as much beer as I could. Everyone loved me.

A woman put her tongue into my mouth and claimed that she could feel the pig's eyes dancing up my throat. I took off my bathing suit to show everyone the hard-on she had given me.

When I tried to swim in the ocean, my brothers tied me to a beach chair that tipped over sometime in the night. A security guard from the Hilton Hotel found me the next morning. I was naked and still tied to the chair. The police were called in.

I told the two officers that Martians had landed and taken me hostage. I explained how I was forced to have sex with an alien life form and that I might be the father of strange, deformed creatures.

They told me to go home. They did not want to see me ever again.

The hit television show *Hawaii Five-O* was filmed on our island. With my brothers gone and my mother and the Captain busy with their dogs, I decided my life's goal was to be a movie star. Fame and fortune might make me a few friends. I convinced Barney to try to be an extra with me. We got up at 4:30 one morning and went down to the set at five. There was already a long line of HBC and Polynesians, the type the show usually used. We stood in line. I had my father's flask. Barney deserted me long before eight o'clock. He was going for the attendance award our school gave every year at graduation and didn't want to ruin his record.

James MacArthur, a.k.a. Danno, walked by and asked me if I wanted to make a buck.

"A little more would be more like it," I told him. Extras on the set were paid fifty bucks for standing around looking Hawaiian.

"This is something special," he said.

I told him he looked exactly like the guy on the show.

He called a cab and gave the driver directions to a private resort on the other side of the island. I had a message for a woman in the ambassador suite.

"Follow that car," I told the driver as I made myself comfortable in the backseat. "There's something in it for you : step on it."

The driver told me he'd beat the shit out of me if I

up. "I got enough of a headache without a smart-alecky kid in my backseat."

"The hair of the dog usually works wonders," I advised.

We stopped at the gas station and parlayed Danno's money into a six-pack of beer. We drank it fast, burping as we drank more. He cheered up. We bought another six before getting back on the road. We stopped twice so I could piss. The third time he wouldn't even slow down, but made me pee out the window. I soaked my jeans. The smell of urine is not that different from the smell of cheap beer.

The woman who answered the door wore a white nightgown that touched the tips of her feathery sandals.

I told her I could smell sin in the air.

She would not let me in until I told her I had a message from Danno.

"Why doesn't the scumbucket call me himself?"

"The phones on the set are down."

"You got an answer for everything, little buddy?"

I considered this question, but didn't know how to answer so that it would work to my advantage.

She went to the dresser and stood in front of the mirror looking beautiful. She pushed her hair on top of her head and pinched her lips as if she planned to kiss someone. She studied herself carefully, turning her head first to the left, then to the right.

I told her she was a real tomato.

"I need to slap the shit out of a man," she said and let her hair drop. It was blond and fell past her shoulders.

"Vengeance is mine," she lisped at me, and I realized I wasn't only early-morning drinker in the room.

e told me to wait outside while she packed. I hesitated, gave me two twenties to do what she said. I made more money that day than I did in two years' pickpocketing from my mother and the Captain.

The cabdriver had fallen asleep in the parking lot. The sun had moved, and his face was sunburning in wide, clown-like stripes. I shook him awake and asked how fast he could get us to the airport. He was the kind of man who drooled when he slept, and a large dark stain had already formed on his shirt sleeve.

I sat in the back and asked the woman if she'd make out with me. It was a long drive to the airport, and once you saw one palm tree, what was the point of seeing another?

"Would you mind shutting up for a minute or two?" she purred at me. She had overdone it with the lipstick, and her two front teeth were stained bright red.

The cabdriver told her that was about as likely as the skies raining dollar bills.

They dropped me off at the television set.

"Tell Danno I said go to hell," she said.

"Anything you say." I saluted her and told her that maybe next time she was in town we could make the earth spin.

I walked past the security guards and marched straight up to Danno. I told him he was worry-free.

"Don't tell me you got her off the island?"

"You know it," I said.

He flashed me a grin, all teeth, and I knew he was pleased with my actions. We slapped palms like old buddies.

"What can I do you for?" he asked.

I knew how fickle Danno could be. Each new episode came with a set of new friends for Danno. Each new show brought case of new concerns.

I told him what I wanted.

Me and Danno Booking Titi...

"I think they've already got somebody for the...
told me.

"I was a fool to do your dirty work," I said.

"Gimme a minute," he said and went over to discu...
ity cards with the two camera men. He was h... & in s...
"It's all yours," he said and patted me on the back. "Stand t...
tree and practice your lines."

We did the scene in three takes, and everyone on the ...t burs...
into applause when I said what I had to say.

"Book 'em, Danno," I winked straight into the camera. The
director yelled "Cut."

It was a wrap.

I was in heaven. The cast and crew congratulated me.

Another volcano must have erupted in Mauke, for that night,
when I got home from my big TV filming, my mother announced
that she and the Captain were no longer seeing eye to eye
on the poodle business. She and I were moving to the mainland. She was going to work beside her sister at Mama Bear's
Country Kitchen in Titusville, Pennsylvania. We were going
to live in a brick house with my aunt and five young cousins.
Every Sunday we would *visit* my grandmother in Oil City
and eat boiled chicken, canned corn, and iceberg lettuce with
French dressing. I would *drink milk.* I would wear shoes and
socks, and just as soon as she *found* the time, Mom would drive
me down to the K-Mart mall and *buy* me my first pair of winter
boots.

She kissed me and told me animal *hair*dressers were an odd
... "I like pilots," my mother said. "Roving *eyes.*"

...onvinced my mother had lost her *mind,* I fled to Barney's
... and camped under his porch, calling *on* any god who
...sten.

more money that day than I did in two years' pickpocketing from my mother and the Captain.

The cabdriver had fallen asleep in the parking lot. The sun had moved, and his face was sunburning in wide, clown-like stripes. I shook him awake and asked how fast he could get us to the airport. He was the kind of man who drooled when he slept, and a large dark stain had already formed on his shirt sleeve.

I sat in the back and asked the woman if she'd make out with me. It was a long drive to the airport, and once you saw one palm tree, what was the point of seeing another?

"Would you mind shutting up for a minute or two?" she purred at me. She had overdone it with the lipstick, and her two front teeth were stained bright red.

The cabdriver told her that was about as likely as the skies raining dollar bills.

They dropped me off at the television set.

"Tell Danno I said go to hell," she said.

"Anything you say." I saluted her and told her that maybe next time she was in town we could make the earth spin.

I walked past the security guards and marched straight up to Danno. I told him he was worry-free.

"Don't tell me you got her off the island?"

"You know it," I said.

He flashed me a grin, all teeth, and I knew he was pleased with my actions. We slapped palms like old buddies.

"What can I do you for?" he asked.

I knew how fickle Danno could be. Each new episode came with a set of new friends for Danno. Each new show brought a case of new concerns.

I told him what I wanted.

"I think they've already got somebody for the end shot," he told me.

"I was a fool to do your dirty work," I said.

"Give me a minute," he said and went over to discuss my acting career with the two camera men. He was back in seconds. "It's all yours," he said and patted me on the back. "Stand by the tree and practice your line."

We did the scene in three takes, and everyone on the set burst into applause when I said what I had to say.

"Book 'em, Danno," I winked straight into the camera. The director yelled "Cut."

It was a wrap.

I was in heaven. The cast and crew congratulated me.

Another volcano must have erupted off Mauke, for that night, when I got home from my big day filming, my mother announced that she and the Captain were no longer seeing eye to eye on the poodle business. She and I were moving to the mainland. She was going to work beside her sister at Mama Bear's Country Kitchen in Titusville, Pennsylvania. We were going to live in a brick house with my aunt and five young cousins. Every Sunday we would visit my grandmother in Oil City and eat boiled chicken, canned corn, and iceberg lettuce with French dressing. I would drink milk. I would wear shoes and socks, and just as soon as she found the time, Mom would drive me down to the K-Mart mall and buy me my first pair of winter boots.

She kissed me and told me animal hairdressers were an odd lot. "Like pilots," my mother said. "Roving eyes."

Convinced my mother had lost her mind, I fled to Barney's house and camped under his porch, calling on any god who would listen.

"I lift my heart to the sky. I give my heart. I give my heart. I give my heart," I pleaded.

I was Danno's right-hand man. I was on my way. I was not just a star, I was the light that shone from it.

The nights were cold. I snuck into their house and drank their cooking wine, which made me throw up. My mother visited me under the porch, and I told her I had an allergy against moving to the mainland.

My mother packed our house in one afternoon. The real estate agency came over with their FOR SALE sign, which I immediately took down and threw into the ocean. The house sold without it, and before I knew it we were on our way.

Titusville, Pennsylvania, was just as my mother described it. I drank rum-and-cokes and walked around my aunt's house in my cousin's ski parka, a wool scarf wrapped around my head. I wore my multicolored mittens to all meals.

Everyone ignored me.

No one had seen the *Hawaii Five-O* episode.

My aunt told my mother that the apple had not fallen too far from the tree. I was one bad nut, she said when she bought the lock for the liquor cabinet.

I sat on the back porch in three feet of snow and smoked packs and packs of cigarettes, careful to save all the ashes in plastic milk containers. When spring came, I borrowed the neighbor's garden hose and took my supplies to school to show my classmates what it was like to live on the islands of Hawaii. My teacher had been trying to get me to participate in this activity since my arrival in late October.

I dumped the ashes into one end of the garden hose, then stood on the teacher's desk and asked my classmates to close their eyes.

"Pretend I'm a small island," I instructed. No one closed their eyes. They sat and stared at me as blankly as they stared at the teacher. "Chant," I told them. "'I give my heart to the sky.' Chant it three times to be saved from danger."

The room was silent, and the teacher asked me if I wanted a slide projector. Perhaps I had some photographs of the islands I could pass around. Hadn't my mother and I brought any leis to share with my new friends? I hushed her with a long hiss, then put the end of the hose into my mouth and blew the cigarette ashes onto the classmates who had never bothered to speak to me.

My father's flask was in my pocket and I sipped from it, making the noises I imagined one heard during a volcanic eruption. The class screamed. Some kids covered their heads, others ran from the class. The teacher demanded I stop. "Get down from there, you," she shouted. "You. You. You," as if I didn't know who she was talking to.

But an eruption doesn't stop because someone wants it to. I spouted the remaining ashes over the room, finally getting the attention I had been looking for.

I was expelled immediately, no questions asked. They didn't care to hear my explanations. My mother tried to believe it was God's will. My aunt said if she had it her way, I'd be shipped back to the savage island I had come from.

With nothing else to do with my days, I went down to Rowling Randy's Bowling Room and sat on the end stool. It was dark and the television in the corner was tuned to *The Andy Griffith Show*.

"You ever get *Hawaii Five-O*?" I asked.

He didn't answer or seem interested in what I had to say, but I told him anyway. I told him twice. Then I told the guy with the goatee who bought me beers. We switched channels all afternoon looking for my moment of glory and television fame.

"Me and Danno." I crossed my fingers. "We were like this."

They nodded, obviously impressed.

"I should have stayed on that island," I told my new friends. "I could have been someone. I really could have been someone.

"Yep," they agreed. "That's right."

We all agreed with each other about me.

It was nice and warm in that room. I took off my sweater and unbuttoned my shirt. I showed my new friends my fading tan lines.

I've been belly up to that bar ever since.

Figures on the Shore

A SOFT RUMOR MOVED ACROSS MARQUETTE that winter. In the dead of January, most people were hibernating and not listening to town gossip. Still, the news that a mysterious boat had docked in the lower harbor late one night passed slowly from the men at the fish house to the lottery lady at Doc's, then on to the gas station attendant, who told the snowplow removers, until finally Janeene heard it from her mailman. Yannick Murphy, the only eyewitness, claimed to have counted fifty people sneaking off the boat. Dressed like Eskimos in long fur coats and heavy boots, they walked single file along the breakwater until they got to shore, where Yannick lost track of them in the dark quiet streets. They spoke French, and Yannick was certain they were Canadians. Their conversation sounded clandestine, he reported, as if they were planning something dangerous.

Lake Superior had not frozen that year. The cold weather

snapped every few days, allowing the warmer temperatures to melt the thick ice formations that extended from the shallow waters close to shore. Some mornings the deep blue lake sparkled like sapphires, making it impossible to look at anything without squinting. Then suddenly the wind would push in heavy winter clouds, changing the horizon to a solid mass of gray. All memory of sunlight gone.

Janeene and her husband, Phil, were newcomers to the area. Not understanding how the winters affected the people of the Upper Peninsula, Janeene believed everything she heard about the mysterious boat. One night, just as they were going to bed, she saw the sharp, angular movements of a deer outside the front window and knew that someone must be hiding in the cluster of evergreen trees. Something had frightened the deer into motion.

"Are you afraid?" her husband asked. "Do you think those people are going to harm us?" They had recently moved from Detroit, and Phil wanted her to feel safe in their new home. He wrapped his arms around her waist and kissed her gently on the top of her head.

"No," Janeene said and believed this to be true. She simply wondered who they were, where they had come from, and why they were hiding in Marquette. She tried to talk to her neighbors the few times she saw them, but they were rarely out. Mostly she relied on her mailman. He was the one who told her how the boat had sunk moments after landing. Janeene invited him in for coffee, hoping to learn more about these strangers. Instead he began confusing things. One day he told her that Tori Anderson had seen some of the boat people in the grocery store buying large quantities of meat and dairy products. The manager of the IGA found forty-seven dollars in Canadian bills in the cash drawer, but neither cashier remembered or would admit to taking the money. Later when Janeene asked the mailman what time Tori had seen them, he looked startled and told her he had no idea what she was talking about. She knew he slipped whiskey into his coffee mug when he thought she wasn't looking, and after he had forgotten what he told her for too many days, she decided it was best to stop asking him in. She didn't want to worry about him getting drunk and walking down the narrow sidewalk paths. She worried he would fall. He could lie hidden behind the waist-high snowbanks for weeks before anyone found him.

Phil was amused by her fascination with the town gossip. He was the kind of man who believed he could protect his wife from anything. He took pride in their marriage and considered their relationship different from and better than anyone else's.

"It's us against the world," he would tell Janeene when something upset her. "We've got to stick together." Phil's assurances always sounded like warnings, and she stopped telling him when she had had a bad day. Coming home from dinner parties or nights out with friends, Phil would discuss the things that were wrong with each person they had been with. "Carl's too concerned with making money to pay any attention to his marriage. Denise is too wrapped up in Carl's life to see that she is wasting her own." Janeene understood what Phil was talking about, but also knew she would not have noticed these things on her own.

They had decided to move north the previous year when Phil's mother died. An only child, Phil inherited money from his father's dry-cleaning business, which had expanded into five stores in the northern suburbs of Detroit. The interest on the inheritance was enough to support them, and without the need to work, there was no reason to stay in Detroit. In September they rented their two-bedroom condominium and moved into his family's vacation home in Michigan's Upper Peninsula.

Phil thought it was the perfect time to start a family. They

had been married six years—their love was obviously secure—
and now they had money and time to devote to children. Phil
had been subscribing to the Marquette newspaper for a year and
told Janeene that it was one of the safest cities in the world.
There was some crime—teenagers shoplifting at the mall, cars
stolen from the deer camps—but only one murder had been reported in two years. Phil studied the case carefully. A twenty-
two-year-old man had been found in Presque Isle State Park.
The police told the newspapers that someone from the iron-ore
ships had robbed and killed the young man. That rumor didn't
last. The hospital in town was the largest employer, and word got
out that the man had been gutted. The victim was a homosex-
ual, and the people of Marquette, if not the police, were certain
that some kind of homophobic local had committed the murder.
They did not believe the crime was as random as the police insisted. Phil, used to the crime rate in Detroit, did not consider
this incident something that could change his mind about raising his family in Marquette.

"Gutted?" Janeene read the article after Phil told her about
the case. "What does that mean?"

"Like you'd do to a deer," Phil explained. He ran his hand up
her stomach to her throat and splayed his fingers across her
cheekbone. "The guy's insides were taken out."

Janeene asked if there were any photographs of the body.

"Would you look at it if there was one?" he asked.

"I don't know." She swatted at his hand as if his touch bothered her.

Although she was hesitant to tell Phil, Janeene did not want
a baby. She did not want one growing inside of her, and she especially did not want to care for one. She continued taking the
pill even though she told Phil she had thrown them away in August. Since their move north she had stopped coming when they

made love. She knew she did not have to reach orgasm to conceive, yet she thought that if they both came during sex it would be something greater than it was, which might somehow lead to a baby. This was something she did not want, so she refused to share her desire with him.

Since neither of them was working and since they had so much free time, they made love often. It was frustrating to hold back, and Janeene longed for the late afternoon, when Phil went jogging. Finally alone in the house, she would escape to the upstairs bathroom. There were days when she couldn't wait for him to get out of the house before she began touching herself. She would stand in the bathroom, her fingers covered with lotion, waiting for the slam of the front door. If the feeling was intense enough, she'd start rubbing herself, often reaching orgasm just as Phil called out good-bye. Then the house would settle around her breathing. She would do it again. This time on the bed without her clothes. It never took more than a few minutes until her body would start shaking with an incredible need that seemed to get more desperate the longer they lived in Marquette.

She always kept her eyes closed. Either afraid or embarrassed by the act, she was not comfortable watching herself get excited alone. Afterward she would rush to do something physical like scrub the bathtub or wash the kitchen floor—anything so she didn't have to think about what she was doing.

Having money without working was strange for both of them, and Janeene wondered how long they could keep up with the simplicity their days presented to them. Like on a vacation that continued long after it should have, they seemed to be waiting for something to happen, for someone to tell them that it was time to go home.

They still got up early—the same time as when they worked in the main office of the dry-cleaning business. Instead of going anywhere, they made lists of chores to do around the house, even though these were things they would finish by noon. In the early afternoon they'd walk down the street to the diner and order grilled cheese sandwiches and french fries covered in hot gravy. The waitress called them dears and filled their coffee mugs so full that the thin brown liquid poured over onto the matching saucers.

Afterward they'd walk to the Peter White Library so Janeene could read the *Detroit Free Press*. She had never been particularly fond of Detroit until the move north, but now she wanted to hear everything she could about the city. Phil spent his library time looking for books on Michigan. His grandparents were from the Copper Country, one hundred miles north of Marquette, and he was interested in learning more about the history of the region. He read a book a night and told Janeene trivia about the region. The world's only marble lighthouse was in Livingstone County. The water flowing over the Tahquamenon Falls was a dark root-beer color because of the iron ore deposits in the land. They made plans to visit these places in the summer. Janeene much preferred talk about traveling around Michigan to talk about the family Phil wanted.

"This is good," Phil told her one night while reading his book. "I'm happy here. He looked up from his reading, his index finger holding his place on the page.

"It is peaceful," Janeene agreed. She did not turn from the window.

"My father should have sold the business when he was alive," Phil said. "He deserved to enjoy life like this."

Janeene nodded, though she wasn't sure she agreed with Phil's enthusiasm about their decision to leave Detroit. She wanted to know what they would do if they simply lived off the money someone else had spent his life earning. Who would they become?

She sat backward on the couch and drew a circle design in the fog her breath made on the windowpane. There had been no news about the strangers for weeks, but she still believed the rumor as strongly as she had when the mailman first told her about the boat docking. Therefore she was not at all surprised to see two men walking up the shoveled path toward the house. She stood quickly, and when Phil asked her what was wrong, she told him there were people at the door.

The men stood on the top steps dressed in orange Day-Glo jackets, the kind deer hunters wore. The air was bitter cold, but they seemed unaffected by the wind or the freezing temperature.

"Our car broke down," the younger man said, and Janeene knew as soon as she heard him speaking English with the tonality of the people from the U.P. that they were not from the boat. She was at once disappointed, as if she had been cheated out of something she deserved.

"We need your phone," the older man explained and then stepped inside without waiting for permission. In Detroit, they would not have answered the door unless they were sure they knew who it was, but here, so far north, with the weather the way it was, the two men seemed as harmless as snowmen. They introduced themselves as Henry and Wade, and when they both took off their hats and stuffed them into their jacket pockets at the same time, Janeene asked if they were father and son.

"There's no use denying that," Henry winked at her.

"Something I've been trying to do my whole life," Wade interrupted. They did not look so much alike—Wade's hair was white blond like a child's, his father's was graying. It was the way they stood—back swayed forward as if proud of their low thick stomachs—that gave them away as family.

"Yours was the only house lit on this whole block," Henry told Phil. Small chunks of snow fell from the tops of his boots.

He shook them onto the carpet, where they stayed in perfect round shapes as if they could ignore the warmth of the house.

Janeene looked out the window to check on her neighbors. They never seemed to be home, but she had no idea where they would be at this time of night in Marquette.

"We've pissed away enough time," Wade told his father. "Let's not spend the rest of the night yammering on about nothing."

"No reason to be rude." Henry seemed happy to be in the house. "You've got to talk to people. You don't just barge in and start using their phone without saying hello. These are the kinds of things that separate us from being animals."

Wade told him to get moving and call Bob's Boron up the road.

"Ignore my son," Henry told Phil and Janeene. "He's not used to being around nice people."

Wade pushed his father as if he could physically force him to the telephone. Henry lost his balance and tumbled into Phil.

"I'm sorry," Phil apologized and backed further into the corner.

"You didn't do anything," Henry said. "This one's the bonehead." He swatted at Wade with an open palm.

Phil offered to make the call, but Henry and Wade seemed more interested in arguing than getting anything done about the car.

"Boron's closed down two years ago," Henry insisted. "The building's already been bulldozed."

"The station in Ishpheming is closed. This here's Marquette. Nothing's been bulldozed around here."

"I know where we are." Henry said. "Sleeping Beauty's the one who's been sawing logs since we left Munising." He closed his eyes and made exaggerated snoring noises.

"At least I was sleeping sober," Wade said and then turned to

Janeene and asked her for a phone book. She told him they didn't have one. Marquette, especially in the winter, was not that big a place. She said she thought the gas station on the corner of Third and Front was open until midnight.

"Do you hear that?" Wade said. "Now go call so we can get someone to jump that thing."

"She doesn't know what she's talking about," Henry argued back. "I've known Bob every year I've been on this earth. Who would know better than me how long he's been out of work? Hell it's probably been longer than two years. Probably closer to three."

"It's always the same with you, isn't it?" Wade asked. You're like some kind of broken record. A goddamn broken record." He made a circular motion with his hand, imitating a record moving round a turntable.

"You're talking garbage," Henry said.

"You just have to be right. About everything. Even if it's none of your business."

"You don't know my business," Henry told him.

"If you say something's blue then it's just got to be blue. Even if everyone else in the world says it's green. You say blue. Blue. Blue. Blue. Blood vessels popping all over your face, you keep insisting on blue. No one's listening to you. No one cares about your goddamn blue. But you won't give up—will you, old man?"

"What in the hell are you talking about?"

"I'm talking about you."

"You got no right to talk about me."

Henry leaned forward and punched Wade, but his balance was unsteady and he missed. The sound they made in their throats was low and raw, like dogs breathing as they circled each other.

Wade moved away from Henry, but Henry tried another

punch. This time he stumbled and fell. Janeene didn't see Wade touch his father, but wondered if he had tripped him.

"Get up, old man," Wade dropped to his knees and straddled his father's body so that his father couldn't move. "Get off this floor. This isn't your floor. You can't be sitting all over it when it's not even yours."

Henry shifted his weight forward onto his elbows, but as soon as he tried to get up, Wade pushed him down. They played like kids on a seesaw.

"Say you're wrong," Wade said. "Say you don't know what you're talking about."

"You're a lunatic," Henry shouted back. "I don't admit to anything."

"Say it," Wade insisted.

"Lunatic," Henry shouted.

"One last chance," Wade threatened. "Just one last chance."

"Get off me," Henry kicked at his son and his pants tore open. He spread his legs and showed them all the long split running up the length of his inseam. The exposed flesh of his inner thigh was bright pink, burned from the wind and cold.

"Now look what you've done," Henry yelled and slapped his son. This time Wade didn't strike back. He laughed instead, which made Henry even madder.

Janeene felt like she had front-row seats to a show she shouldn't be watching. Their fighting, which had seemed so childish when they first came here, was now real. She was thrilled by the strength and anger of their fight.

"How am I going to get home with my pants like this?" Henry tugged at the ripped material, showing the loose skin of his thigh. "Take a good look at what you've done."

"I'm not the one who ripped your pants," Wade shot back.

"You're the one who didn't want to waste the night in Marquette," Henry argued back. "I can't go outside like this. I'll freeze my ass off."

Wade asked Phil if they could borrow a pair of pants. "Nothing special," he said. "Just something for this drunk to wear home."

Phil said he'd go look for something and then motioned for Janeene to come with him. She knew he didn't want her alone with these men, but she didn't want to leave. She liked their arguing, however stupid it was. It was such a relief to be around people—to have something to listen to besides silence. Phil waited, and she knew she had no choice but to go with him.

"This is ridiculous," Phil complained once they were out of earshot. "They're drunk and I don't want them in the house. We should call the police."

Janeene checked the ragbag for something Henry could wear, but all she found were some old beach towels. The multicolored material was so out of place that it took her a moment to remember what the towels were used for.

"He can't go outside with that rip in his pants," Janeene said.

"He outweighs me by fifty pounds," Phil argued. "What's going to fit him?"

"It's the jacket. He just looks big," Janeene said. "You must have something he could wear."

Phil told her to wait there, but as soon as he went upstairs she went back into the living room, where Wade was still sitting on his father. They were engaged in some sort of silent stare-down, neither of them moving or speaking.

Phil came down with a pair of his grandfather's pants—light-colored wool trousers. He handed them to Henry, who thanked him with a nod of his head. Wade continued staring at his father.

Henry unzipped his pants and Janeene told them she'd wait in the other room while he changed.

She poured herself a glass of brandy and sipped it slowly. It was not something she drank very often, but the medicinal taste was somehow comforting and she finished the glass in three swallows.

"What's wrong?" she asked. Phil had the trousers under his arm, his face tight with disapproval and impatience.

"They're too tight to get over his ankles."

"Do you have another pair?"

"Not that I'm going to give him," Phil said. "These will fit if I open the cuff a bit. They're baggy enough for him."

He flipped the scissors off the pegboard and sat at the kitchen table.

"They're just like the people from the boat," Janeene whispered suddenly. "Coming out of nowhere in the middle of the night like this." It was not quite ten o'clock, but daylight seemed something foreign, something they might never see again.

"I can't believe you're still listening to that nonsense," Phil said.

"What do you mean?"

"All the stuff about the boat," he said. "I'm so sick of that nonsense."

"It's not nonsense. Yannick Murphy saw them." Janeene was surprised by Phil's tone. She knew he was uncomfortable with these men in the house, but there was no reason to take his anger out on her.

"Yannick Murphy says he saw fifty people getting off a boat and you believe him?"

Phil made a small cut in the material and began to pull. The pants were thick and difficult to tear.

"People don't make up things like that." Janeene leaned across the table to help, but Phil shoved the pant legs off the table, where she couldn't reach them.

"You ever stop to ask yourself what Yannick Murphy was doing in the lower harbor at two o'clock in the morning?"

Now she was irritated. She had already told Phil the story of Yannick walking home from Doc's Saloon. Drunk, tired, and cold, he was more surprised than anyone to see the boat skimming the dark water as it slowed to dock in the quiet night. The breakwater was icy and he set out to warn them to move the boat to the marina. That's when he saw all the people getting off the boat. That's when he heard them talking and knew that something was up—something strange was about to happen.

"He spent the night in a bar and you're going to believe what he says?" Phil said. "People see all kinds of things when they're drunk. Flying saucers. Seven-footed animals. Mystery ships."

"Maybe you're the one who's afraid," Janeene said. "That's why you don't want to believe it could happen. Because you're afraid of them."

"I'm not afraid of something that doesn't exist." Phil pulled at the material with both hands, and this time it gave way. It caught the side seam and ripped all the way up to the crotch. They were no better than the pair Henry was wearing.

"I don't have anything that's going to fit this guy." Phil threw the trousers to the floor.

"What about something else of your grandfather's?" Janeene would not fight with Phil. Not with these men in the house. "All that stuff we found when we moved in?"

Phil nodded but did not get up from the table.

"Do you want me to look?" Janeene asked.

"No," Phil said. "It's not insulated up there. I'll go."

"A little cold's not going to kill me," she said.

"What?" Phil turned to her.

"Nothing," she shook her head. "Nothing."

When he left, she picked up the trousers and turned them over her arm until she had rolled them into a ball. She was angry that Phil was so upset. It wasn't as if the men had interrupted them. It wasn't as if they were doing anything important when the men came knocking at the door.

She knew they would talk about the men after the tow truck came and jump-started their car. Phil would be relieved that they were gone. He would sit on the edge of the bed and talk to her even after she told him she was tired. He would keep talking even when she closed her eyes and pretended to be asleep. All talked out, he would crawl under the covers and want to make love. Janeene, not finding a reason to say no, would go through the motions.

The thought of the empty house and the days ahead with nothing to do, no one to talk to except Phil, got her so frustrated that she shoved the wool pants into the dirty dishwater just as Wade walked in the room. He did not ask her what she was doing.

The dinner plates had been soaking since six o'clock. Janeene buried her hands up to her elbows and turned the heavy wool in the dead soapsuds while leftover bits of pork chop and mashed potato floated to the top of the still, gray water. She tried to act like nothing was wrong, but she felt foolish taking her frustrations out on a pair of pants.

"You and your husband don't look like you're from around here," Wade said quietly. She fished the pants out of the water and hung them over the side of the sink. The excess water dripped onto the floor.

"We just moved here in September from Detroit," she said.

"You must be going nuts."

"I've never been around this much snow," Janeene said. "It gets cold in Detroit, but nothing like this. Some nights I can almost hear the temperature falling. It just keeps getting colder. I think the wind's going to pull the house down with it." She was out of breath from speaking so quickly.

"I didn't mean the weather," Wade said, and Janeene asked if he was talking about the people.

Instead of answering, he picked up the bottle of aspirin, but his fingers were too thick to open it. He stuck it in his mouth and tried with his teeth.

"Do you have a headache?" she asked.

"I'm not sure." Wade handed her the bottle. The cap was wet from his spit. She turned it until the two arrows pointed at each other, then popped it open with her fingernail.

"Feel my forehead," he said, "and you can tell me if I'm sick."

His skin was soft and warm, but she could not tell if it was feverish. She started to pull her hand away, but Wade held her wrist with a firm grip. He was not hurting her, but his touch made her nervous. Her fingertips brushed the corners of his eyes and he closed them. His lashes were darker than they should have been with his hair so blond.

"What are you doing there?" Henry yelled and Janeene dropped her hand and shoved it back into the dishwater.

"I'm not doing anything," Wade said and turned to face his father.

"She wouldn't touch someone like you unless you bribed her," Henry yelled at Wade.

"He's got a headache," Janeene interrupted. "He doesn't feel good."

"You don't know what you're talking about, old man," Wade said. "Stay out of what you don't know."

Their heavy bodies were not used to the heat in the house, and the smell of their perspiration was everywhere. The strong, stale odor was strange in the winter world, which kept everything so sterile, and Janeene found it unnerving.

"He didn't make me do anything," Janeene said. The pants had dripped onto the floor and she tripped on the wet tile when she started to leave the room.

Wade held her hip and asked if she was all right. She could feel the skin bruising beneath his touch.

Henry smiled at them. "Well. This is cozy," he said. "And you with your husband just up the stairs."

Janeene was still holding Wade's aspirin. She put them on her tongue and then turned to the sink and cupped water into her hand. The aspirin dissolved in her throat, the chalky substance creeping back up into her mouth. She turned and spat them into the dishwater.

"Excuse me," she apologized and went upstairs to see why Phil was taking so long. He was not in their bedroom. The spare bedrooms were cold and dark, and she opened the attic door and called up the steps.

"Phil?" There was no sound. She called his name again, but her voice echoed back to her. She slammed the door and hurried downstairs, wanting to get away from all the emptiness.

Henry was sitting on the couch watching television. He was wearing a pair of dark green pants she didn't recognize but knew they must have been among Phil's grandfather's things. She turned down the sound on the TV and asked Henry where Phil was.

"Like that's something that you're concerned about?" Henry smiled.

"Of course I'm concerned," she said. She wanted Phil there with her.

"Don't give her a hard time," Wade said. "Tell her where her husband is."

Henry kept staring at the television, but pointed to the front door.

"He left?" Janeene asked. "Why? Where would he go?"

"He's getting his car started to give us a jump."

"What about the gas station?" Janeene said. "Couldn't they tow you?"

"The truck's out in Big Bay," Henry said. "They're not sure when it'll be back."

"It's a bad night to be out," Janeene said, and Henry laughed.

"They're all bad nights to be out." Henry zipped up his coat and pulled on his cap until it covered his ears.

"No sense in all of us getting cold," he said. "You two might as well stay here where it's warm."

Wade stood in the middle of the room looking out the window. She knew he was standing too far from the glass to see anything but his own reflection. Yet he was concentrating as if he could see into the night.

He was silent for some time and then slowly, as if coming out of a trance, turned and asked if she was afraid of living in Marquette.

"What would I be afraid of?" she asked.

"Things. All kinds of things go on in these parts," Wade told her. "There's lots to be afraid of."

"Like what?"

"Like ghosts," he said. "Aren't you afraid of ghosts?"

"What do you mean?" she asked. "Like something haunting my attic?"

"I'm talking about people coming back from the dead," he said.

"People don't come back from the dead," she told him.

"They don't?" Wade looked at her, his eyebrows raised. "You know that for a fact?"

"Why would they come back?" she asked.

"To settle the score," he told her. "They might want to get even."

He was trying to tell her something. He had been trying to tell her something all night. The taste of copper filled her mouth, and she swallowed hard to get rid of it. "Did you kill that man in the park?"

"Is that what you think?"

The wind was cold by the open door, but she didn't move. The icy blasts ran up her spine. Her skin spotted with goose-bumps.

"We're hunters up here," he said. "Gutting a deer is something we all know how to do. Those are the kinds of things we learn when we're twelve."

"This is a strange place," she told him. Her voice sounded distant, as if it belonged to someone else.

"You'll get used to it," Wade said. "After a while you'll get used to it." He had been scratching his skin under his shirt, and suddenly, as if he'd had enough of the discomfort, he unbuttoned the top buttons, exposing a large red shape on his chest. It looked like a tattoo—an undefined drawing she didn't recognize right away—but when she stepped closer, she saw that it was a scar. The skin was unmarred, with no hair, like a baby's.

"What about the people from the boat?" she asked.

"They could have killed him, too," he told her. He turned to face her head on as if proud of this mark.

"No. I want to know what they're doing here," she said. "I meant what are they doing in Marquette?"

"Why should I tell you?"

"Because I want to know what happened to them," she said.

"Will you tell me? Will you tell me what happened to those people?"

"No," Wade pulled away.

"Why not?"

"Because," Wayne rubbed the scar as if her touch had made him sore. He buttoned his shirt and turned toward the front door, where they saw Phil making his way up the front walk. Her heart raced as he stepped inside. She grabbed the edge of the table and held tight to stop the dizziness taking over. The room seemed to be losing light, as if Phil had carried the night in with him.

Phil's glasses fogged, and he set them on the table. Janeene reached for them so that she could wipe the condensation off, but her hands were clumsy and she pushed them onto the floor. Phil bent to pick them up.

"Are you okay?" he asked, and she nodded.

"Did you figure out what was wrong with the car?" Wade asked.

"Nothing," Phil said. He put his hands to his mouth and blew on them and then got the flashlight out of the drawer.

"There's nothing wrong with the car? Nothing at all?"

"Not that I can tell," Phil said. He tested the flashlight. The strong light hit the opposite wall and filled the room with long shadows.

"I think your father ran over something," Phil told Wade. "The car started up right away. It didn't need the jump. There's no other reason you would have stalled out."

"Did you see anything?" Wade continued rubbing his chest through the thick layers of winter coat he was not wearing.

"It was probably a deer," Phil said. "A deer's got the strength to stop a car like that."

"Did you check the grate?"

"There was nothing," Phil said.

"Then it wasn't a deer," Wade told him. "Deers leave their fur."

"There was nothing except a dent near the driver's-side head-light," Phil said.

"There'd be blood if it was a deer," Wade said. "Those animals bleed more than any animal on this earth." They stood, ready to leave the house.

"Wait," Janeene called as they went out the front door.

They turned back and looked at her. "What?" Phil asked.

"I want to see it. I want to see the car," she said. She put on her coat and wrapped a wool scarf around the bottom part of her face.

"It's thirty below out there," Phil said. "Stay in here where it's warm."

"There's no reason for you to be out on a night like this," Wade said. "This kind of cold can kill you."

They were gone before she could protest further and right away the silence of the house was overwhelming. She closed her eyes and took a deep breath, trying to let go of whatever it was that was scaring her. The panic increased, and she stepped outside and stood on the front porch, letting the wind run through her body.

Phil and the men huddled around the two cars, but she could not hear their voices. She did not know if they were talking to each another. Phil had pulled his car around so that it faced Henry's, and the front ends touched like animals confronting each other.

She turned toward the lake and saw a flash of light shoot up from the ground. She stared into the darkness, and a few minutes later there was another flash. Certain that it was not her imagination or something in the sky, she stepped off the porch. Staying close to the houses, away from the street lamps, she walked as fast as she could through the snowdrifts. When she was far enough away so that the men would not hear or see her, she took off.

She ran stiffly in her heavy winter clothes. The cold air filled her lungs, and her sides ached with cramps. The fear stayed with her, but she refused to stop. She had to know what was out there.

The breakwater was somewhere off to her left. She could hear the rustling noise in the tall evergreen branches. It was too dark to know exactly where she was until she reached the beach. The winter wind had caught and trapped the sand like waves in motion. She turned to look where she had come from. Marquette was covered in a shadowlike net cast from the lake. It was near midnight. The streets should have been deserted, yet she thought she saw shadows moving in the distance. If there were only a bit more light, Janeene was certain she would at least see hints of all the figures hiding on Superior's shoreline. But understand them, she could not.

Women Drinking
Benedictine

THE WAY MY SISTER EXPLAINED IT WAS THAT she wanted to get rid of her husband. I never believed she'd really kill him, but she was definitely up to something. She claimed she was going about it slowly, not because she was afraid of being caught, but because she loved Randy too much to use rat poison or to blow him away with the 30-caliber rifle he's got hidden between the washer and the dryer in the basement. Instead Siobhan was relying on a series of small accidents—accidents that in time would make him leave her. Last fall she loosened the lug nuts on his car tire. She pictured the tire flying off as he was driving down the highway into Munising. Luck just had it that the next time he drove the car, the Holsum Bakery truck in front of him ran over a squirrel. Randy had to slow down to keep from smashing into the rear end of the truck, and that's when the tire fell off. He was only going about ten miles an hour, so it wasn't anywhere near the accident it should have been. He plowed into a tree and broke his collarbone and two of his ribs. The hospital kept him overnight to get all the windshield glass out of his face, but it wasn't anything worse. As Siobhan said, that one should have been the one.

Siobhan said being married was not for her. She was tired of the way things were, and she wanted a change. I know what it is to be trapped in a dead-end situation, and I wanted to help her get out of it. Getting rid of Randy wasn't going to solve anything, but you can't argue with Siobhan. She gets angry and she'll snap like a dry twig in the woods. That's why it was up to me to interfere with her plans. Whenever the attempts on Randy's life didn't foul up of their own accord, I had to step in and rescue him.

Yesterday Siobhan stayed up until four in the morning putting together a booby trap in the bathroom. She hadn't warned me about this attempt. When Randy closed the door, the garden tools wrapped in the bedsheet were supposed to fall on his head and kill him. But he was standing over the toilet taking a leak when he kicked the door shut. The rake knocked a gash in his forehead, but it didn't come close to killing him. It got him acting dizzy, and he wandered out onto the highway without realizing who he was or where he was going. Siobhan was asleep, planning to wake up a widow, when the hospital in Marquette called to let her know they had sewn fourteen stitches into Randy's forehead. A road construction crew had found him wandering on I-41 just south of Munising. He was resting comfortably and Siobhan could pick him up after his observation period—anytime after 12:00.

"You were going to do it in the house?" I should have guessed Siobhan was up to something; she'd been unusually quiet the last couple of days. "What were you going to do with the body?

Drag it outside?" We haven't had the snow we usually get, but I still couldn't see Siobhan acting like that in an emergency.

"Of course not," she said. "As soon as I got up I was going to call the state police. They would have gotten rid of it."

"How were you going to explain the rake and the snow shovel on the bathroom floor?" It was hard for me to imagine why Siobhan wanted to be single, especially in Munising. Everyone we know is married with kids.

"I was going to put those back in the garage," Siobhan said. "Right back where they belong."

"Don't you think the police would have asked you how he was killed? They might be interested in how he died, you know."

"Oh, stop," Siobhan said. "You act like it's some big mystery, like there'll be an investigation with magnifying glasses and police reports."

"If he's dead there will be."

"It's March." I could hear her sigh. "Do you know that? It's already March." Randy was supposed to have been dead by Christmas so that Siobhan could begin the New Year a single woman. We didn't talk about what she would do as a widow— how it would change her life or anything—but I liked my part in Siobhan's plans. She's the kind of person who can make anything exciting, even life in Munising.

"Do you think they're going to let you get away without even a mention of how Randy got himself killed on his bathroom floor?" I never could figure out how Siobhan thought she would get away with murdering Randy. It just didn't make sense.

"My God," Siobhan swore. "I know just what will happen. I can see the whole scene in my mind. Burns and Anders will come screaming up the driveway in their patrol car with the siren blaring away. Then they'll see Randy dead with his head smashed in and they'll start carrying on and soon they'll be crying and telling me what a good friend and fine man Randy was. The neighbors will start flocking out on the front lawn, staring at the house like they never saw one before, all of them asking stupid questions, and one of them, probably Mrs. Saxon, who doesn't like me anyway, will knock on the door with a ridiculous plate of her dumb macaroons, and just when I turn my back, Burns will find the whiskey under the sink and in no more than fifteen minutes, my clean kitchen will be filled with nosy neighbors and everyone will be putting on a drunk so bad that maybe, just maybe, one of them will sober up by the end of the week, and by that time no one will remember how Randy died, but everyone will be too stupid to ask anyone else."

Kate's my baby and she was crying while Siobhan was going on. I put her back in her high chair and fed her the rest of her breakfast—oatmeal and canned peaches. She eats it three times a day. When I try to feed her something else, she starts scream-ing. Nothing else keeps her quiet. I work during the day and Siobhan looks after her. She tells me Kate's a fine eater. I don't argue with her or say any different. I figure Kate's getting her protein with Siobhan and her fruit and fiber with me. We get along best when she's not crying, so I don't force her to eat any-thing that makes her upset.

"You watch out, Siobhan," I warned her. "You might not be as smart as you think you are."

"This isn't Detroit," Siobhan said. "Women don't go to jail in the Upper Peninsula."

"Aren't you forgetting about Maureen Bogden?" I asked. Kate was busy playing with her reflection in the stainless steel part of the baby chair. Siobhan didn't say anything, so I re-minded her of the time Maureen Bogden caught hold of a rumor that her boyfriend was sleeping with the part-time waitress from the Dogpatch. No one had any proof of it, but as soon as Maureen heard the news, she marched herself into the Dogpatch and knocked the waitress in the jaw. The Munising police arrested Maureen right there in the bar, in front of the band and everything.

There was a silence on the other line and I thought Siobhan must have been mulling over my warning about Maureen.

"Siobhan, are you listening to me?" She didn't answer, and all I could hear was silence coming over the line.

"Siobhan?" I said louder. "What's wrong? What is it?" Something bumped against the receiver on her end, then I heard her voice loud and clear.

"Sorry," she said. "I had to go to the bathroom."

Kate started crying, and I removed the silver tray to lift her out of the high chair. She stopped crying when I set her on the floor.

"I had three cups of coffee," Siobhan said. "I couldn't wait."

"You should tell me when you're leaving the phone," I said. "I was saying something."

"I'm listening to you." Siobhan started to snap a bit, but she caught herself before she yelled at me. She was careful to be nice to me, and I thought it was because she liked having me as her partner in crime. "I listen to everybody."

I finished the rest of Kate's breakfast and then ran water in the empty dish. It would soak with the rest of the breakfast dishes.

"Did Kate stop crying?" Siobhan said.

"She's fine," I said. "She'll be asleep in about a minute. Just about time for her to nap again."

"Why don't you bring her over?" Siobhan said. "I'll watch her and you can go down and pick up Randy."

"What's this?" I asked. Siobhan usually gets me to go with her when she has to pick up Randy. After the bowling accident failed, the three of us went to the Brownstone Inn and played darts until two in the morning. Randy could play fine with his broken toes. He shot from his bar stool and scored higher than both me and Siobhan.

"Please," Siobhan begged. She dropped her voice and let the words drag out. "I can't talk to Randy. Not just yet."

"Why don't both of us go?" I said. "We can go together."

"I can't do it," she said. "How am I going to face him in Marquette with people looking at me? Those people are nurses and doctors. They'll know something's wrong."

I didn't say anything.

"Please do it for me?"

She didn't have to put it like that. It's not like it's any big deal to drive to Marquette. I go there all the time. Kate's father is stationed in Marquette—up at K. I. Sawyer Air Force Base. I drive up once a month to get the support checks. Since we're not married, I'm not allowed on base, but he drives out to meet me at the Roadhouse right where County Road 551 connects with 41. It feels good to get out of town and see some new faces. On Thursday nights the Roadhouse has what they call adult entertainment, and the place jumps. The girls aren't as good-looking as I thought they'd be. Everyone stares when they first take off their tops, but after a couple of minutes there's nothing to look at—nothing changes. Pretty soon everyone's back playing pool or watching the TV, and the girls end up dancing in their corners by themselves.

Siobhan must have been waiting by the window, because she came running down the front steps when I drove in. The yard and the house looked normal enough. I remember the time I went over there after the hunting incident. Randy and his buddies were heading out to Michigamme to shoot rabbit, and Siobhan emptied out all the kerosene in their cooking stoves. She pictured Randy starving to death out there in the woods. I was nervous about that one, but no one was even suspicious.

"Go on back inside," I said. "Kate's buckled in her car seat. It's going to take a couple of minutes."

"Let me do it." Siobhan gave me a push with the side of her hip, and I stepped out of the way.

"Is everything okay here?" I took another look around the property. "Did you put the rake and shovel back in the garage?"

"She's adorable," Siobhan said. "You know I think she's precious, don't you?"

"Remember, I'm going to be bringing Randy home in a couple of hours. I want to make sure he's not going to suspect anything."

Siobhan lifted Kate out of the backseat. "We're fine here. Just fine." She held out her hand for Kate's day bag of diapers and an oversized stuffed choo-choo train. The blue-and-white striped train is a present from Siobhan; Kate never plays with it at home, but at Siobhan's she seems to love it. I find her in the middle of the living room floor pulling the train in circles and laughing when it tips over. She screams when I have to pack it away, but when we get home she won't even look at it.

I started to follow them into the house, but Siobhan turned around and told me that I should get going.

"I thought the hospital wasn't going to release him until noon," I said. "There's still an hour to get rid of."

"You don't want to be late." Siobhan had Kate balanced on her hip, and the day bag was over her shoulder. She's taller than

I am and doesn't look cluttered with all of Kate's stuff. "The roads might be icy. That's a bad stretch of highway there."

Siobhan was right about Highway 28 getting icy. There's nothing but a few pine trees to block Lake Superior, and the wind comes straight across with the speed of all that open space. But the weather had been still that week—the same heavy gray sky hanging over us for days.

Siobhan gets moody after the accidents, so I left without complaining about her rudeness.

It was a Saturday, but the streets felt empty. Munising had been upset with a pack of strangers the past two weeks. A whole team of cameramen had come up from Detroit to film a Kawasaki snowmobile commercial. They brought fifteen snowmobiles and about that many stuntmen. The guys rented out ten rooms at the Best Western and were bothering everybody in town. Two of them dressed up in a bear costume and walked into the Dogpatch trying to scare away the locals. I heard the bear outfit was part of the commercial they were filming. Supposedly a guy drives one of the snowmobiles into a cave. It comes tearing out the other end, but the guy's gone and there's a bear driving the machine. They've been hanging around town so long because they're waiting for fresh snow. Someone asked them how long they plan to wait and they laughed and said, "How long does it take for the snow to come?" Someone should tell them we've had snow as late as May up here.

I drove to the Dogpatch and checked out the cars in the parking lot. Denny Kennedy's red-and-black LeMans was parked by the side of the building. He's an old friend from high school and he sometimes picks up an odd shift at the Dogpatch. He and the owner have been drinking buddies for years.

There wasn't any sun that day, but it still took me a few minutes to get used to the yellow light. Denny was sitting behind the bar leaning forward on his elbows. He didn't move a muscle when I walked in.

"You hung over, Denny?" I pulled out one of the stools and sat in front of him.

"Not too bad." He held out his hand, palm down. I could barely see his shakes.

Everybody says there's no hope for Denny. His father was an alcoholic—only made it out of Munising to die in a dry-out clinic in Arizona. Denny's the same way. He told me a person doesn't know what a real drunk is until they've shit in their pants. I asked him how many times that had happened to him and he laughed. "No use counting," he told me. "There aren't no reason in the world to keep track of a thing like that."

There's nothing wrong with the way Denny looks. Most of the girls in town have had a crush on him at one time or another. A few of us have even slept with him, but most nights he gets too drunk to be horny. I'd help him if he'd let me, but he doesn't seem to need anybody.

Denny reached over and grabbed two mugs from the cooler. "Drink a draft with me?" he asked. He didn't have to move to reach the taps.

"I'm going to Marquette," I said.

"Heading up to the base?"

"Straight into town," I said. "Randy's got himself in another one of his accidents."

The beer was cold, but the glass tasted of dishwashing soap. They got an automatic glass washer for the Dogpatch, but the bartender forgot to empty out the peanut shells before they washed the ashtrays, and the machine broke a week after they bought it. Now they just rinse out the glasses in a sinkful of soapy water and let them dry on the bar.

"It's pretty hard to believe." Denny finished the draft in a couple of swallows and picked mine up to refill it. I told him I wanted a bottle of Canadian Blue.

"Sure is," I said. "It's hard to believe one man can be so clumsy." Denny was smelt fishing with us the night Siobhan tried to poison Randy with grain alcohol. We had made a campfire up on the north shore waiting for the smelt to run, and Siobhan was mixing the cocktails. It was damp, the early spring winds were cold, and we had to drink a lot to keep warm. She made our drinks with Popov vodka, but Randy's were lethal, pure alcohol she bought from some woman who brews her own.

Halfway through the night, Siobhan started complaining about being bored, so Randy suggested that we go on home. She took both sets of keys and the guys were stuck out there. Siobhan pictured Randy dying of exposure, but fluke of all flukes, Denny stayed somewhat sober that night, and he remembered an old cabin one of his friends had out there. They broke in and spent the night protected from the wind. The doctor told Siobhan the alcohol actually saved Randy's life.

"I'm not talking about Randy," Denny said.

"Then what's so hard to believe?" I had considered telling Denny about Siobhan and her plan to get rid of Randy. He's someone who would understand about why she was doing it and about why I was helping her. But I never did. He's not sober too often, and I didn't want to get him in any trouble if she ever did manage to carry it off.

"There were two women in here this morning," Denny nodded to the dance floor. There was a table in front of the window and I could see a few dirty glasses and some bar napkins crumbled in the ashtray. "Two beautiful, beautiful women."

"What women?"

"I don't know who they were." Denny grabbed the string of my purse and pulled it over to his side of the bar. He knows I don't smoke, but he still rifles my purse for cigarettes every chance he gets. "You wouldn't believe what they looked like," Denny said. "Incredible. They didn't look real. But I know they were. I could hear them talking and laughing like real people."

"What'd they look like? Martians?" I asked.

"They looked like they walked off a page of a magazine. Makeup on and everything."

"You didn't know them?" I asked. "And they came here alone?" The Dogpatch isn't the kind of place that people who don't know the area would come for a drink.

"They were right there. Bigger than life. More beautiful than any life I've ever seen." He pointed to the dirty table again, only this time I didn't turn around.

"God, they were beautiful." Denny finished looking through my purse. I made sure my wallet and car keys were still there and then dropped it over the arm of the stool.

"They didn't have stomachs," Denny said. "They were all flat here." He leaned over the bar and put his hand on my stomach. I was wearing long underwear under my sweater, so I couldn't feel his hand. I know I'm not fat, but I still had weight on from having Kate and I didn't like Denny looking at me like I was heavy.

"You could put your hand around their waists," Denny said. "I swear to God, one hand would fit around their waists."

"Do you think they were from downstate?" I asked.

Denny ignored my question. "Do you know what they ordered?"

This time I looked over at the glasses. They weren't beer mugs so I guessed Bloody Marys.

"Benedictine."

"What?"

"Benedictine."

"What does that mean?"

"It doesn't mean anything. It's a drink."

"And those women wanted to drink it?" I kept looking at the table. There was no ice in the glasses. I could see straight through them to the dirty window and then the brick wall.

With a great effort Denny got up and walked the length of the bar. His body tilted and he dragged his heavy right boot. Denny doesn't have a heel on that foot and has to wear a support boot. The accident happened two springs ago during the Au Train canoe races. A bunch of people were drinking down by the finish line, and Denny was sitting on the hood of Bruce Pelke's VW. Bruce got in and started to pull away. He thought Denny would jump off, but Denny was too wasted to know that they were moving. He fell off the car, and his ankle got tangled in the front bumper. For a while they thought he was going to lose his whole foot. Now when he gets really loaded he'll take off his socks and show how the ankle is sewn right to the arch of his foot. But when he's got his clothes on you can't really tell anything's wrong except that he walks funny and sometimes stands way over to one side. The alcohol doesn't help the way he looks; I think it makes it worse.

Denny set the heavy bottle in front of me, but I didn't really care about looking at it. I was making my plan of what I would say to Randy. It's one of the reasons I like helping Siobhan with her attempts. It gives me something to concentrate on, something to worry about so I don't go winter crazy. Denny pulled out the small cork, then put the bottle to my nose.

"That's different," I pushed the bottle away. The smell didn't burn like whiskey, and it wasn't sweet like schnapps.

"Want some?" Denny flipped down a shot glass and tapped it on the bar.

"I've got to go. Randy's out of the hospital at twelve." It felt good to have a plan, to have something to do with the rest of the morning and part of the afternoon. I figured we'd end up back at the house and play euchre that night.

Denny tilted the bottle and drank a sip. "Come on," he said. "Be a beautiful woman and drink Benedictine with me."

"I don't want to." I got up and zipped my jacket. Denny took another sip from the bottle. He must have had his mouth open too wide, because some of the liquor dribbled out the sides and ran down his shirt.

"I'm going to find those women," Denny said.

"Be careful, Denny," I said.

"Yep. That's what I'm going to do. As soon as my shift ends, I'm going to go find those women."

I shook my head and Denny raised his voice.

"Just you watch me," he said. "The minute Bob comes walking in that door to take over, I'm out of here. I'm going to find those beautiful, beautiful women."

"You go right ahead," I said. "And then you tell me what you're going to do once you find them."

Denny set the bottle down and picked up the cap. He bit into the corkscrew and I thought he had gone back to his daydreaming. But just when I got to the door, he shouted, "I don't have to worry about that right now. I've got to find them first."

The guys at the pool table looked at me, even though it was Denny who was shouting. I ignored them and gave Denny kind of a half-wave good-bye.

Randy was standing out on the sidewalk in front of the revolving doors when I pulled into the hospital's circular drive. He was wearing blue-and-white hospital pajamas, so I figured he must have been wandering on the highway without a shirt. I stopped the car but forgot to put it in neutral, and when Randy opened the door the car rolled forward.

"I'm sorry. I'm sorry." I set my foot on the brake and the car jerked to a full stop.

"Give me a minute, Caroline." Randy slammed the door. He had a large white bandage on his head and his skin smelled like hospital soap.

"I'm sorry," I repeated. "How're you doing? You feeling okay?"

"I'm going to live. It's just a few stitches this time," Randy said.

"You don't look too bad," I said.

"Where's Siobhan?" Randy bit off his blue hospital bracelet and threw it on the dashboard.

"She's home watching Kate."

"Is she okay?"

"Siobhan?" I looked at him to see if he was making some kind of a joke, but he was as serious as he always is.

"She's fine," I said when he didn't answer. "Just fine."

"That's good. It's good that she's with the baby," he said. "She loves that baby."

"She does love Kate," I decided to go along with what he was saying. "There's no question about that. She loves her an awful lot."

Randy put his head back on the seat, but I was glad to see that he kept his eyes open. He might have had a concussion, and you're not supposed to go to sleep with one of those.

The wind was coming off Superior with more force than on the drive in. I kept two hands on the steering wheel to stay on the right side of the yellow line. The sky, one continuous piece of gray, looked like it was moving in closer to snow.

"She gets so upset," Randy spoke without opening his eyes. "I feel horrible when she's upset."

It was hard to imagine what Randy was talking about. It sounded like he knew about the attempts on his life. I had wondered this before. Randy's not stupid and he's not clumsy, though I tell people he is because of the accidents. It's hard enough to explain how often he gets hurt.

"It's my fault and I don't know what to do about it," Randy said. "I'm absolutely helpless and that makes it worse."

"You're helpless?" I didn't believe this. Siobhan may be determined, but if Randy told her what he knew, she would quit with the accidents and maybe see about a divorce. She'd have to.

"Completely."

"Why don't you stop her?" I asked. The straightaway was turning into the bend by the lake, and at that angle my eyes got trapped in a pocket of brightness. I squinted to block out some of the light.

"You can't stop desire, Caroline," Randy said.

"Don't let her do it," I argued. "You can stop her."

"Siobhan's wanted this forever," Randy said.

"So what?" I said. "She's always getting what she wants. Who says she has to get her way this time? A lot of us don't get our way. Why should Siobhan be any different?"

"I guess I want one, too," Randy said. "I know I don't deserve one. It's my lot in life, but I want a baby, too."

The brightness was getting worse. There wasn't a drop of sun, but the reflection off the snow and the lake made looking at the road impossible. I cupped both hands around my eyes and kept the car steady with my knee. There weren't any cars on the road. Randy leaned over and put his hand on the steering wheel. He kept the car straight until we moved into the shadow of the pine trees near Au Train. And just the way he was acting, so calm, so understanding, I knew we weren't talking about the same thing. We weren't talking about the same thing at all.

"You want a baby?" I said. My eyes were tearing from the light.

"More than anything," he said.

"And that's what Siobhan wants?"

"I know that's what she wants. I knew Siobhan wanted babies when I married her," Randy said. "I just loved her too much to tell her that I didn't have the stuff."

"What stuff?" I asked.

"Besides," Randy kept going. "I wasn't 100 percent sure. But I am now."

"Really?" I said. "How can you be so sure?" Randy was breathing heavily, and for a minute I thought he was going to have an attack.

"Do you think these accidents are just a coincidence?" Randy asked.

"No," I said. "I don't think they're a coincidence at all. Not at all."

"Christ, all we do is try to have babies," Randy said. "I can't help being clumsy and forgetful. I'm worn out. I'm tired all the time now."

"You've been trying to have a baby?" The car swerved off the blacktop and I could hear the tires running on the gravel. I pumped the brakes for about a mile and then slowed to a full stop. Randy didn't panic. I guess he had had plenty of practice with near accidents.

"That's all we've done this year," Randy said. "I mean all we've done. We don't even play cards anymore."

"Siobhan wants a baby, too?"

"More than anything," Randy said. I was starting to feel funny. Those were the exact words Siobhan used when she talked about wanting Randy dead. She told me she wanted him out of her life more than anything. That's how she'd said it.

"We have sex so much that it's starting to make me sick. One night we tried fifteen times. I was so sore, I wanted to pull it off."

The traffic light in the middle of Munising was green our way, but the cars in front of us were backed up almost to the end of town. I slowed down, thinking the cars would start moving through the intersection, but they just sat there and I had to slam on the brakes. The inside of the car was hot, and Randy's hospital smell was making me breathe through my mouth.

"It's the snowmobile people," he said. "They're going out across the lake that way." He pointed over the dashboard toward Superior.

I didn't need Randy to make any reports. I could see the line of snowmobiles crossing the street as clearly as he could. Their engines roared together and the noise shook the street.

"I thought Siobhan had talked to you about this," Randy said. "You're sisters. I thought she told you everything."

"Well, there are some things you don't know." He sounded like he was sorry for me and I didn't like that. It was one of the reasons I had agreed to help Siobhan in the first place. I liked being included in her plan. At that point, I thought about telling Randy a thing or two. I felt like telling him that I had saved his life a few times, but when the last snowmobile crossed the street and the cars started up, I kept quiet until we pulled into their driveway. Randy said he wanted to check on some things in the garage. I didn't even bother getting nervous about the snow shovel and the rake. I figured if Siobhan hadn't put them away by this time, there was no use trying to help either of them.

Siobhan and Kate were sitting under the kitchen table eating peanut butter on saltine crackers when I walked in.

"Siobhan," I said. "Get up from under there."

"Why?" Siobhan asked. "What's wrong with you?" It was perfectly bright outside, but Siobhan had on every light in the house. She says it keeps away the winter gloom, but I tell her that much light isn't good for anybody. I turned off the overhead in the kitchen.

"How come you never told me you and Randy were trying to have a baby?"

Siobhan bent sideways and peered at me through the wood slats of the chair. "He told?" When she tried to stand up she hit her head on the edge of the table.

"You've been wanting a baby for a year?" I was furious that Siobhan had tricked me into believing her.

"I told him not to tell you," Siobhan said. "I knew you'd be furious."

I reached under the sink and got out her bottle of whiskey. It was brand-new, and the cap was still sealed shut. I broke it with my teeth and poured out a glass. The sharp taste made me think of Denny's Benedictine and I drank the full shot, trying not to cringe.

"You lied to me, didn't you?" I asked.

"Not really," Siobhan said. "You never asked me about a baby."

"But you weren't killing him."

I reached for Kate, but Siobhan had her wrapped in her arms.

"Were you?" I asked. "Were you trying to kill Randy?"

"Of course not," she said.

"Never?" I asked. "Did you make up everything?"

"You don't kill your husband," Siobhan said. "They're hard enough to find as it is."

"What about all the accidents?" I poured another glass of whiskey, but when I brought it up to my lips, my stomach wasn't ready for it, so I dumped it down the sink.

"I was mad at him," she said. "I wanted a baby. I still want a baby."

"But I saw Randy get hurt. Those accidents were real," I told her.

"He can't have a baby," Siobhan said. "Randy doesn't have the stuff it takes to make a baby." She held Kate up as if she was demonstrating a science project.

"But you weren't killing him?" I didn't want to drink anymore, but it gave me something to do while I was trying to figure things out, so I drank more.

"No. I told you no." Siobhan tucked Kate's legs into her arm and with her free hand reached for the bottle. "I was just angry with him. He knew what was going on."

"Why'd you lie to me?" I held the bottle away from her.

"I don't know."

"Why couldn't you tell me the truth?"

Siobhan turned away and started picking up Kate's train set. The engine was stuck on something under the table. The material stretched, and she kept pulling on it until it gave way. "Because you got so excited about it," she said. "You just seemed to get a kick out of it."

Randy came walking in the side door and startled me. I had forgotten all about him. Siobhan leaned up and kissed him right below his bandage.

"Did you ask her?" Randy asked.

"Why'd you tell her about not being able to have a baby?" Siobhan asked.

"I thought she knew," Randy said.

"Ask me about what?" I stopped pouring out the whiskey and looked over at Siobhan. "What were you going to ask me?"

"Nothing." Siobhan took the stuffed train and walked out of the kitchen. Randy called her back.

"Not today," she yelled from the living room. "Don't say anything, Randy. It's not a good time."

"Tell me," I said. "You've got to tell me now."

Siobhan came storming back into the kitchen and started fuming about the wasted liquor. "What are you doing with my whiskey? You're not even drinking it."

"So what?" I said. "I want to know what's going on." I held the whiskey bottle over my head and started pouring it down the sink.

"All right, all right." Siobhan grabbed the bottle, but I hadn't let go, and she spilled more pulling it away from me.

"The thing is," Randy said. "We'd like to have Kate."

"What do you mean?" I could see a line of blood running down Randy's nose. I pulled off a section of paper toweling and handed it to him. He wiped the peanut butter off Kate's face and then tossed it in the trash bin.

"We want to adopt Kate," Siobhan said.

"Kate's mine," I said. "She's my baby."

"We know that."

"Well, you can't just adopt her." I was angry that Siobhan had used me. All these months and she had never really needed me. She had been lying to me all along.

"But we'd like to," Siobhan said. "That's what we're trying to tell you. We want to make her part of our family."

"I'm her mother."

"Right. But she needs a father." The three of them stood there looking at me as if everything had been decided without me.

"Her father's on base. It's only forty minutes down the road," I said. "That's a lot closer than some fathers I know."

"But Randy could be her father right here. Right now."

"She's too young to want a father now," I said.

"Babies need fathers," Randy said. "They need them even when they're as young as Kate."

"How do you know?" I asked.

"We've asked people," Randy said. "I've been talking to a lot of doctors, and they say a baby knows when she's not in a family situation."

"That's not true," I yelled. "You don't know that. You don't know anything about babies. You can't even have one."

Siobhan was into her smug routine and didn't even react to my comment. She was pretty sure of herself, just like she always is, like she'd never get punished for lying to me.

I couldn't take looking at the three of them. I tore out of the house and drove down the driveway at forty miles an hour. It was a stupid thing to do, because they had Kate. I got to the end of the driveway and put the car into first gear, but I just didn't have the energy to start fighting with them again. I turned around and headed into Munising, figuring that they could worry for a change. I'd let them worry about when I'd be back for Kate.

The hills were casting just enough of a late afternoon shadow that I didn't see Denny right away. I caught a glimpse of something moving on my side of the road, so I slowed down and then kept staring into my rearview mirror until I recognized his silver jacket. It was Denny all right. I could see his uneven boots from that far away. I pulled off and walked back to where he was standing.

"What are you doing?" I asked.

"I know where my women are." Denny seemed happy to see me. He was holding a bicycle—an old two-wheeler with no gears. "I've discovered who my beautiful, beautiful women are."

"Who?" I was still crying, but Denny didn't notice.

"Think about it," Denny said. "It all makes sense."

"I don't get it." I was fed up guessing what people were talking about, but Denny didn't play the game for long.

"They're models with Kawasaki," he said. "They're up helping film the commercial."

"So what's with the bike?"

"I can't believe I didn't think of it sooner," Denny said. "You should have thought of it too. You're a smart one. You could have put two and two together."

"It's only March," I said. "What the hell are you doing with a bicycle in all this snow?"

"They're shooting the commercial on Grand Isle," Denny said.

"So what?" I asked. "They've been shooting that commercial for the last two weeks."

"I can't take a car there. It'll go through the ice."

"You're going to ride a bike there?"

"I have to find them," Denny said. "I just have to see them again."

"You'll never make it." The sky was dusky, and the clouds were getting lower and lower as if sometime during the night they would simply touch the snow to the ground.

"I've got to make it." Denny stepped over the bar and got on the seat. He tried to move the pedal forward, but his bum foot was too weak to pull it around.

"You'll get caught in the dark soon." I grabbed hold of the handlebars to help support the bike.

Denny kept kicking at the pedal, but he wasn't getting it, so I bent down and moved it into place. He tried pedaling forward a few inches and stopped in front of the snowbank.

He seemed satisfied with his short ride. He put the bike over his shoulder and carried it to the edge of Lake Superior. It was all ice, impossible to tell where the beach ended and where the water started. Denny was panting, but as soon as we got to the lake he got back on the bike. He tried pedaling again, but he was having a hard time because his boot was too big for the pedal. He rode for a second before he had to jump off. The bicycle slid on the ice and spun away from him.

"For God's sake, Denny." I went over and grabbed the bike. "Be careful." I dragged it back and held it out to him.

"I need your help." Denny sat on the ice, not making a move to get up.

"No way," I said. "It's too cold to be out here."

"Please, Caroline," Denny said. "Pedal the bike for me."

"What are you talking about?" I asked. "What good is it going to do if I take the bike to Grand Isle? Where are you going to be?"

"You can ride me," Denny said. "I'll go here." Denny stood up quickly and moved to the front of the bike. He stretched his arms out behind him and threw his leg over the front tire. He boosted himself up and sat on the handlebars. The bike shifted, and I had to lean forward to hold him up.

"Do it, Caroline. Please. I can't do it by myself."

"You don't need me," I said.

"I do," Denny said. "I really need your help."

"Do you mean it?" I put one foot on the other side of the bike. My feet could easily reach the pedals.

"Of course I do," Denny said. "Remember this morning in

the bar when I told you I was going to find those women? Well, that's what I'm trying to do now. That's all I want to do now. I just want to find my women."

The wind picked up and started moving across the open bay, making it hard to hear what Denny was saying. He had worked up a sweat carrying the bike to the lake, and his hair was wet. He licked the sweat off his upper lip and stood there, just looking at me and waiting to see what I would say, and I decided I might as well help him.

"This is crazy," I said.

Denny let out a yell and we started up slowly. He wasn't very heavy, but the ice underneath the thin layer of snow was slippery and it was hard to keep both of us steady. I couldn't keep the bike balanced when I was sitting, so I stood, keeping the dark line of pine trees and the red blur of the lighthouse in clear sight, and I pedaled Denny all the way to Grand Isle to find his women.

Awaken with My Mother's Dreams

HE FAMILY BLAMED ME WHEN MY mother tried to kayak over Tahquamenon Falls last spring. It was a stupid and dangerous stunt, and they thought that I had somehow encouraged her to attempt the fifty-foot drop. The waterfall, the second largest east of the Mississippi, is in Michigan's Upper Peninsula outside a town called Paradise. My mother knew the area from books she read about Michigan rivers and campgrounds and was well aware that, at maximum flow, fifty thousand gallons of the Tahquamenon River roar over the precipice every second. It was only the first day of April, but the temperature was close to fifty degrees when she unloaded her plaid-bottomed kayak and put off just above the tongue of the river. The root-beer-colored water, overflowing and cold, tumbled onto land as it made its way out to Whitefish Bay in Lake Superior, and my sisters, Nina and Megan, were convinced that I had helped plan my mother's so-called suicide run.

"You might just as well have given her a bottle of Elavil or locked her in the garage with the car running," Megan said to me over the phone after the police had called to inform her of the "accident."

I told her I was in a hospital and couldn't hear her.

"Tied the noose around her neck," Megan yelled. "Put her head in the oven and held it there."

"You don't know what you're talking about," I said.

"Don't I?" Megan shouted. I held the phone away from my ear as if to solicit complaints, but the hospital was empty of people that afternoon.

"No. You really don't," I said, then hesitated, since there was no sense denying that I had spent the last few days vacationing with my mother in the Upper Peninsula. We had left Detroit early Wednesday morning full of plans for a spring camping trip. My mother insisted on bringing her kayak even though a late March storm had recently dumped ten inches of snow over the entire state. This was nothing unusual—no reason to panic. My mother had been taking her kayak with her ever since those first lessons in the pool at Schoolcraft Community College two years ago. Since then she had conquered local rivers, even won a trophy for her Indian rollovers in rapid water. We had tied the awkwardly shaped kayak to the roof and had driven slowly in traffic around Detroit. The highway cleared as we got farther north, and we would have forgotten all about the kayak except for the bow, which hung over the windshield casting elongated, almost animal-like shadows on the road in front of us.

"You helped her plan this, and then you sat back and watched her do it." Megan was starting to repeat herself. "We're talking about the woman who gave you life, the woman who brought you into the world."

"Don't be so dramatic, Megan." I could see my mother's

room from where I stood. She was asleep. They had not sedated her. She was simply exhausted. The nurse had already assured me that her concussion was minor, and except for a few signs of frostbite near both big toes, she was fine.

"The police told me that no one has ever made it over the Falls." Megan was at work. She's an environmental engineer for General Motors in suburban Detroit. She sometimes wears a hard hat and drives a golf cart when she goes out to new sites. The plant was loud, and Megan often comes home hoarse from shouting over the roar of machinery. Things were quiet on her end of the line that day, but she was furious with me, so she was yelling.

"They said no one tries it," I said. "It's illegal," I said "There are signs everywhere warning you that you'll be arrested if you try it."

"So what was wrong with Mom? Couldn't she see the signs?"

"That's why she did it," I explained. "Because she knew it was illegal. She wanted to be the first." A siren started up outside. I twisted the phone cord in my fingers and pulled the receiver to the window. A few seconds later the noise subsided. Perhaps a false alarm.

"They would have found her body out in Lake Superior," Megan said. Her voice caught and I could tell she was crying. I told her I was sorry.

"There are just so many times when I can't believe that you're my sister," Megan said.

"Yes," I said. "I know." Megan and I are only a year apart, but we have never been as close as we pretend to be.

A few minutes later we hung up. Megan and my younger sister, Nina, were leaving as soon as they could. I had lost my wallet months before and had never bothered to replace anything. Since I had no I.D., the police wouldn't believe I was related to my mother. They didn't think she was quite right in the head and wanted someone from the family to be with her.

My mother was still in shock when the DNR guys dragged her from the river. I think she rolled over on purpose just as their motorboat approached the kayak. She would never have allowed them to tow her in to shore with that odd-colored rope they threw her. She must have hit her head on a rock, maybe on the bottom of the kayak, but she quit fighting and they pulled her to the far shore. The thick-planked cedar footbridge was wet with the turbulent spring waters, and it took me some time to cross over. I knew they could see me. The Day-Glo colors of my windbreaker were visible within at least a three-mile radius—probably more in the thin, gray branches of the new Michigan spring.

Instead of taking her to the local hospital, they transported her across the Mackinac Bridge to Petosky. I think they thought she was really crazy and wanted her to be as close to home as possible. Since I had no license, the police made me leave my car in the parking lot and ride downstate in the ambulance.

"Why not?" I asked when the driver refused to let me sit with my mother.

"You might do something stupid," he told me. "I can't keep an eye on you both." The guy held the steering wheel tightly, as if his grip was keeping us on the road.

"I'm not going to do anything," I promised. "I just want to sit back there so she won't be alone." I didn't want her to be frightened if she came out of shock while we were still in the ambulance.

"She doesn't seem to be the kind of person who scares easily," he told me. "They caught her trying to kayak over the falls. Even the Indians got out and walked around when they heard the sound of rushing water."

I stared out the window at the rainclouds the spring winds were moving in. The storm caught us as we were crossing the Mackinac Bridge. White lightning darted over Lake Michigan while the sky above Lake Huron stayed bright with the disappearing sun.

And though I wanted to believe that my mother would be scared if she woke up in the back of an ambulance, I knew the driver was right. My mother was not this kind of person. I don't know when or why she lost her fears. I don't think it happened all at once. Maybe she watched too much television. She spent so many nights alone in that four-bedroom house in suburban Detroit. After my sisters and I went off to college, my father continued to travel on business during the week and left her alone. The darkness and silence of those empty rooms made her turn to the television for company. She hated sitcoms, and made-for-television-movies bored her. The endings were too predictable, she said, the people too beautiful. One night, flipping through the channels on the remote control, she found the twenty-four-hour sports channel and started watching the Pistons. A hometown team: She got hooked. She loved the emotions of the players, their excitement on the court and in the locker room during the postgame interviews. She was impressed by the players' tears and gratitude as night after night they thanked their mothers, their coaches, their wives, their gods. At first I thought she felt maternal about these young guys, but gradually I came to understand that she didn't want to be their mothers— she wanted to be one of them.

"Your mother likes sports," my father told me a few months before he died. He was in Beaumont Hospital, three days out of intensive care, and these were not the kinds of things I wanted him to concentrate on. The painkillers made him spacey, and he had to struggle to put together a complete sentence.

"I certainly hope they have a good season," he said.

"Excuse me?" I asked. The hospital room was warm. I was wearing my winter coat, and my skin, underneath the thick wool, was prickly and uncomfortable. But there was no place to put it except on the bed, which seemed rude, so I kept it on.

"The Pistons," my father said. "For your mother's sake, I hope the Pistons have a good year."

"Really?" I asked and stared out the window at the skeleton structure of the new hospital wing. The construction workers had finished the top floor. The undecorated Christmas tree stood at the very edge of the building.

"Yes," my father nodded. "I want her to be happy." He did not say after he was dead and I'm not sure that that's what he meant, but I nodded to show him I understood and then he asked me to go to the gift shop and find something for him to read. He was bored, and it was obvious to the family—and probably to the doctors and nurses—that my father saw his days in the hospital not as a time of recuperation but as a time of vacation. He saw them as days when he could catch up on his reading and take long afternoon naps whenever he pleased. He was ignoring his illness just as he had always ignored his health.

This was my father's second heart attack. The doctor had already warned the family that he was not a cat—he could not have another heart attack and live. I wanted to talk to him about the family, to talk about my mother, about what he thought she should do if he died. There was the house, the two cars, the property up north, all those bills, but when I came back upstairs with a bagful of paperbacks—some thrillers, which he hated, some mysteries, which he had probably already read—he started in again about my mother and the Pistons.

"You should ask her about the team. Percentage shots, rebounding records, previous teams. She knows all those kinds of things." He sat up and sorted through the stack of books, obviously unhappy with my choices.

"What if I don't care?" I asked. "What if I just don't care about basketball?"

"We're not talking about you," he said and handed me back half the stack. "This is about your mother. Not about you." His hair was almost all gray that afternoon. I remembered he once told me he wanted me to remember him as a younger man, but now even after I look at photographs of him, I can't remember him without the gray streaks in his hair. "Ask her about the postseason games last year. She watched every game."

I was not living in Detroit at the time and had no idea how important the Pistons or their season would become for my mother. I did not know then that my father would come home from the hospital seemingly healthy, with plans for a new diet and exercise program, only to die in his sleep one night. My mother was right beside him and didn't realize he was dead until she reached across the bed to turn him over. She thought she heard him snoring, but it was morning and he was gone. That spring we were all glad that my mother was interested in basketball. The Pistons kept her occupied and gave us something else to talk about. We thought she'd gradually come to accept my father's death, and there seemed nothing wrong with her obsession with basketball. And that June when the Pistons lost to the Lakers in the seventh game overtime, Isaiah Thomas limping down the court with a swollen ankle, the buzzer sounding way too early, my sisters and I cried with her.

My mother and I hadn't slept much during our camping trip. The nights were cold, and our sleeping bags got soaked with the early dew long before we were ready to get up.

I went into her hospital room and stretched out in the chair beside her bed, anxious for a few hours' sleep. I wanted to be alert when Nina and Megan arrived.

A nurse shook me awake just as I was drifting off.

"That's my mother," I said, hoping she would close the blinds and leave me alone. There was no sun, but the gray light made me cold. I was still wearing the clothes from that morning, and I was chilled. The nurse explained that it was nap time for the hospital—all visitors were to leave. I didn't think I would be disturbing this activity, but she refused my request to stay.

"There's a reception area downstairs," she said, adjusting the blankets around the foot of my mother's bed. "They serve coffee all afternoon."

I took my time putting on my coat, and that's when I saw my mother's wet suit in the trash can. The sleek, black material was already dry, and I held it up for the nurse. "What's this doing here?" I asked. She shrugged and said she had no idea.

"This is her lucky suit," I explained. "The one she's worn from the beginning. She'd never forgive you for throwing it out." I tried several times to roll the suit into a ball, but the rubbery material, used to the shape of my mother's body, would not let me reduce its size. I spread it out on the nightstand, where the arms stretched over the corners of the thin wood dresser, the legs barely touching the floor.

The year after my father's death was hard for everyone. Prompted by a rush of Megan's phone calls, all warning that my mother was losing her mind, I went over to the house one Saturday afternoon in late September to have a talk with her. "Find out what she's doing," Megan directed. "I think we should know what she's up to."

"What makes you think she'll talk to me?"

"She probably won't," Megan said. "But it's worth a try." Megan believed my mother was going crazy with a grief that never seemed to lessen.

I found my mother sitting in the living room eating pretzel sticks and sipping red wine. The radio was turned up. The music prevented her from hearing the back door slam shut when I let myself in. I stood in the kitchen door and watched. She was involved in some sort of conversation with the love seat. She turned her head toward the armchair and smiled. Someone was sitting over there as well. She laughed and made a large circle with her free hand as if illustrating a point. Her lips were painted rose red, the shade she wore when she went out at night. She held the wineglass up to her lips and drew her tongue around the rim. It was a flirtatious movement, and even in her navy blue sweatsuit she looked sexy and pleased with her imaginary cocktail party.

I wasn't surprised to find my mother drinking so early in the morning. I didn't think it meant that Megan and Nina were right, that she was having some sort of nervous breakdown. But I saw as clearly as I ever had the depth of my mother's loneliness. I saw her desperation for company—her longing to be around interesting people—people who were interested in her life and the things she had to say. I had no idea who was at her party, though I hoped my father was there and that they were enjoying talking to each other again. If he wasn't there, then I hoped it was someone intelligent, someone sensitive, who would convince my mother that she was happy—that she had had and was still having a good life.

"I'm drinking because I'm frustrated," she told me later that day even though I hadn't said anything about the wine.

"I'm bored. Just bored out of my skull," she continued. "It's so frustrating to be so bored." I told her she didn't have to account for her actions—that wasn't why I was there—though I suppose it was exactly why I was there.

We talked about what she might do besides drink. The world's largest flea market was at the Pontiac Silverdome that weekend. Mrs. Henshaw, the neighbor from across the street, had been trying to get my mother over for some authentic Icelandic cooking since her return from an around-the-world cruise.

"You should get involved in something," I told her because, back then, I was sure that being with other people would keep her from being so lonely. I suggested volunteer work or maybe working in one of the several retail shops in the area. I imagined her making friends, having them over for tea, planting tulip bulbs when the ground was moist with spring rain.

"I feel like I'm living out the epilogue of my own life," my mother told me. "I've had my husband. I've had my kids. There's nothing left for me to do."

"You're not that old. It's ridiculous to talk this way."

"I'm tired of looking backward," she said. "Tired of remembering everything. But I can't see anything ahead. I don't see much changing in my future." The wine filled her body with black shadows that I could not get rid of so easily.

"Winter's almost here," I said. "And then it will be spring." The day was gray, as it always is in Detroit in October. The trees had lost most of their leaves, their thin bare branches melted into the thick cloud cover. I searched for things I could promise her. "Little Barry will be walking soon. Think what a terror he's going to be once he starts getting around on his own." Barry was Megan's youngest son, ten months old. My mother used to call him her dream child because he was so beautiful.

"Maybe," my mother drifted away from the conversation.

She was staring out the window and nodding as if she were listening to me, though her thoughts were clearly somewhere else. She might have been thinking about her abandoned cocktail party. Outside two squirrels ran in circles around the thick pole holding the birdhouse. Their hyper, energetic behavior kept the birds away, but I suspected my mother threw birdseed on the ground specifically for the squirrels.

"I've already had my kids," she said when she finally drifted back into the conversation.

"I know that," I told her. "All I'm saying is that you have grandkids who love you. They're a part of your future."

"I spent all those years raising my own kids. I don't think I want to do it again."

"You don't have to do anything," I said. "Megan's going to do all the work. She'll take the responsibility for her own kids. You can just sit back and enjoy them."

"I don't think so," she said, and I knew that she wasn't denying her grandchildren or their growing up. She was denying something else, something she wasn't articulating just yet. I poured more wine into each of our glasses, and she drifted back into her daydreams. I turned on the radio and started cleaning up the kitchen. I fried up two turkey sausages, and around noon we ate them with celery sticks and finished off the jug of wine. Sometime that afternoon we decided that a long walk around the neighborhood would lift our spirits.

"I wish I could play basketball," she told me when we were halfway around the block.

"Women's basketball isn't that interesting," I argued. "They can't dunk." I ran ahead, pretending I was making my way down a basketball court toward the net, then jumped for my layup. The leaves on the sidewalk scattered when I landed.

"Then I wish I could be on the men's team," my mother said. She had always been stubborn, but depression made her more so.

"You'd be awfully short."

"Not all of them are as tall as they look." She was wearing a kelly-green stocking cap that one of us had knitted for her in seventh-grade home economics class. The stitches were long and loose, the tiny ball hung halfway down her back.

"Some of them are seven feet tall." I said, but I should have known better than to get into this kind of thing with her. She was much better than my father had predicted before he died.

"Spud Webb's only 5'6"."

"Spud Webb sounds like a potato," I told her. The street lamps flickered on. We were back home, but evening was still a half hour off, and we started around the block again.

"He plays for Atlanta," she said. "Went to school at North Carolina State. But the shortest player in the NBA is only 5'3"."

"That's impossible," I said. It was raining, but the day was warm—almost humid—and we had not bothered with umbrellas. "He'd be a midget out there with all those other guys."

"Tyrone Muggsy Bogues," she said and stopped walking while she collected her thoughts. "He's with the Hornets. Came from Wake Forest. Check it out if you don't believe me."

She knew I wouldn't know where to begin to look up that kind of information.

"Well, those guys might be short, but they're young," I reminded her, not because I didn't think she knew this, but because I wasn't sure how serious she was.

"I didn't say I could play pro basketball. I'm saying I wish I could play it."

"I wish you could play it, too," I told her. "Megan, Nina, and I could be the presidents of your fan club. We'd be there at all the home games holding up signs with Bible quotations no one would understand, screaming out your nickname when you stepped up to the foul line." I sneezed and she handed me a tissue. It was a sign that I should either wipe my face or blow my nose. I did both and then, just as I had when I was a kid, handed her the soiled tissue, which she stuffed back in the deep front pocket of her raincoat.

Later that week, when I called to invite her out to dinner, she told me she couldn't go. She was busy.

"Doing what?" I asked.

"I'm going to learn to kayak," she said, and I asked her to repeat what she had just said.

"Kayak," she said and then spelled it out for me. "Like the Indians did. That's how they saw the world. They got in their kayaks and paddled to different places when they got bored."

"Really?" I asked.

"Yes," she said. "I'm going to have my adventure."

"I see," I said, when at the time I clearly didn't see anything at all.

With nothing to do at the hospital, I took a taxi to the Petosky airport.

The front door was locked, but when I knocked a woman in a ski parka opened the door.

"You caught me napping," she said. Her checks were red, her eyes puffy. I apologized.

"The Blue Goose arrives in an hour." She pointed to the door leading out to the tarmac. The Petosky County Airport has so few flights that instead of numbers they use nicknames. One airline, one gate—the Blue Goose arrives from Detroit at 4:00 P.M. every day, the Canadian Fowl in from Sault Ste. Marie at noon, and the Chicago Eagle at 8:30 every other evening.

Megan and Nina, the only women on a flight with seven businessmen, were last off the plane.

"Welcome to Petosky," I said.

Megan was surprised to see me. "You left Mom alone?"

"She's sleeping," I said. "This trip exhausted her."

"I bet," Megan said.

Nina stood a few feet away from Megan and me. Nina has always been closer to Megan. I used to think it had to do with size—they are exactly the same size and have shared clothes since they graduated from Catholic grade-school uniforms. Even now they borrow each other's dresses, good shoes, winter dress coats. Their lives continue to be similar, just as they were when we were growing up. They both work for General Motors, Megan out in the Lake Orion plant, Nina in an accounting division at the headquarters downtown. They both live in suburban Detroit, and both their husbands are from Indiana, a detail that sealed, at least for me, their similarities. Nina is still debating whether or not to have kids, but when she does, I'm sure she'll have two. Just like Megan.

Nina hugged me stiffly. Her oversized carry-on bag swung off her shoulder and hit me on the top of my right thigh. I could tell she was trying not to be angry with me.

"Why'd you have to do something so stupid?" she asked after Megan was out of hearing range. "Really, Caroline. Doesn't the family have enough to worry about without you doing something stupid like this?" Nina wears the same perfume as my mother, and the musky odor startled me until I got used to it. Then it seemed to underline why we were talking like this.

"Megan's furious," Nina whispered. "She wants to know what happened."

"She already knows everything," I told her. "We talked on the phone for half an hour."

Nina shook her head. "The police told Megan you were standing on the side of the river. They said you let her get in the boat. You stood right there and let her do it."

"Close," I said. I moved my hands apart as if to measure the distance. "I got pretty close. The river is right beside a beech forest, so it's hard to get right up to the river. The state park is a maple and beech tree haven. You'll find more of those trees there than anywhere else in the world."

"Don't," Nina warned and started walking toward Megan and the car-rental woman.

"Don't what?" I followed alongside her.

"Don't do this."

"Don't do what?"

"You treat this like some kind of joke, and Megan's going to explode," she said. "You have no idea how angry she is."

"What about you?" I asked. "Are you mad, too?" The other passengers arriving on the Blue Goose had gone, and the large room was again quiet except for the clicking of the baggage carousel, which had circled with only a few pieces of luggage.

"I just don't know what you and Mom have been up to," Nina sighed, and I knew she and Megan had argued this over and over on the flight north.

"We haven't been up to anything," I said. "No one's been up to anything."

"Sometimes when I'm over at the house I feel like I'm walking into some kind of secret club. All sorts of whispering and planning."

"There isn't any club," I said, but Nina walked away and joined Megan by the door. The woman told me she had enjoyed talking with me, and I thanked her.

The wind was coming off Lake Michigan, cold and sharp, nothing at all to do with spring, when we stepped outside.

"I can drive," I volunteered.

"No." Megan shook her head. "Absolutely not."

"I know my way around," I argued. "It'll be easier than me yelling out directions every two minutes."

"You don't have a license," Megan said. "Remember?"

"Would one of you open the door?" Nina said. She had her hands deep inside her coat pockets, and she looked tired. "I don't care who drives the car. Just open it."

"It's not illegal for me to drive," I said. "I just lost my license. I can still drive." But I handed the keys over and got into the backseat so Nina could sit closer to the heat vents.

Megan drove straight into downtown Petosky without asking for any help. She didn't even hesitate, and I said something about what a good memory she had. As a family we used to vacation in that part of northern Michigan when we were kids. My father rented a two-room cottage on Walloon Lake, and we spent a month there every summer.

I waited in the downstairs lobby while Megan and Nina went up to the room. I was tired but knew I would not sleep.

Megan and Nina don't like the way I live my life. Their disapproval isn't something that makes me want to prove that they're wrong, because I don't think they are. I know my singleness makes them uncomfortable, and they're constantly asking me why I don't date more. This is odd, because I don't date at all. Somehow I imagined my life would be somewhat different from how it actually turned out. I thought by the time I was thirty-three I would have been more settled with my choices. I don't think I counted on a prince on a white horse, but I saw myself with someone. However vaguely I imagined him, I at least imagined he'd be someone.

My mother and I had spent most of our time in the U.P. looking for Indian artifacts. We didn't have any digging tools, but we walked near the shores of Lake Superior, checking near the bases of the tall evergreen trees for things that stood out against the dark-green, dark-brown earth. We were looking for surprises but found mostly rocks and a few pieces of off-white water glass. The man in the pancake restaurant we ate at two mornings in a row told us about shipwrecks in the area, and my mother and I looked for pieces of cargo that might have washed ashore.

"I don't believe other people can keep us from loneliness," my mother said to me one afternoon while we were treasure hunting.

"Well, of course we do," I told her. "That's why we have friends. That's why we spend time with people."

"I don't believe that's true."

"Look at you and Dad. You two were happy together. You weren't lonely when he was alive."

The tall pines moved in the strong wind coming off the lake. We couldn't see it from the path, but the chill of the spring water was in the air all around us, and it burned our faces bright red. My mother stopped walking and handed me something she had hidden in her raincoat. I thought it was a tissue. I shook my head and told her I didn't need one.

"Which one do you like best?" she asked, and handed me two photographs of herself.

"What for?" I asked. "Which one do I like best for what?"

"Oh, I don't know," she sighed. "It's always nice to have a photograph of yourself close by."

She had selected old photographs. Photographs when she was younger. One showed her walking down an aisle in a dark wood church, dressed in a strapless gown with a full skirt. Her partner was wearing a morning suit, gray pants with long dark tails. He was not my father, and when I asked her who it was, she asked me if I liked her hair. I touched the nape of her neck and said it looked fine.

"No. I mean here," she said and gestured to the photograph with her red-mittened hand. "We wore such cute dresses back then. Not like those awful floor-length things you wear today."

"When was the last time you saw me in something floor-length?" I asked.

"Who are you walking with in this picture?" Her dress was nice. Her hair was styled around her face. It was dated, but she looked happy, as if anticipating that something exciting was about to happen.

"I think this one will do." She took the one of her as a bridesmaid out of the plastic bag and gave it to me. "This is really the best one."

"Is that Uncle Bill?" I asked, though I knew it wasn't.

"I wish I had a clearer head shot, but this one will have to do."

"Who's going to need a photograph of you?" My mother was not whimsical. She had a reason for everything she did.

"Keep it in a safe place," she said. "Someplace where it will stay dry." That's all she said, and a few minutes later we went back to our treasure searching. The dead autumn leaves crumbled when we picked through them. The ground at certain spots had thawed, and the earth was cold and wet in our hands. Later that afternoon, we washed the dirt trapped under our nails in the water of the Tahquamenon River, and I began to understand what she was doing.

Nina stepped out of the elevator alone. They hadn't been upstairs long, fifteen minutes at the most. The receptionist was on the phone, her back turned to us. She spoke in hushed tones, but the echoes in the room were such that I could have heard every word if I had wanted to. I stood up and stretched. My lower back ached, and I rubbed it through my raincoat.

"Mom wants to know where her kayak is," Nina said.

"Is she awake?" I asked.

"Awake and worried about the kayak," Nina said. "She's not talking about anything else."

"Does she want to see me?"

"I've been up since five-thirty," Nina complained. "Can you just do what Megan says so we can get some dinner, maybe some sleep tonight?"

Prone to exaggeration, sometimes outright lying, Nina is the kind of person who goes around telling people that her whole life changed when John Lennon died. People are impressed with this kind of statement. It's strong, powerful, almost spiritual, until you add it up. Nina, who was born in 1964, would have been all of fifteen the day Lennon was shot. I once asked her what kind of changes she went through and she said something about cutting out the excessive things in her life. I guess maybe she switched from Coke to Diet Pepsi, or started limiting herself to one hour of television a night. I like her exaggerations and feel sorry when they get her into trouble, as eventually they always do.

"How is she feeling?" I asked.

"She's okay," Nina said. "Obsessed with her kayak."

Up to that point I hadn't been thinking about the kayak. All morning long it had just been my mother and me alone in the park. And then when the DNR guys came out in their boat, it seemed that we were surrounded by people. In all the confusion, I lost track of what happened to her kayak.

"Tell her it's on its way," I instructed Nina.

"What does that mean?"

"Just tell her that," I said. I was sure that the kayak must be in the falls, maybe out in Whitefish Bay by now.

"It's on its way?" Nina asked.

"She'll understand."

"Secret clubs," Nina said and headed back to the elevator. "A two-person sorority. That's what this is."

"Don't worry, Nina," I advised. "Don't worry about it. She'll be happy to hear this."

I found the book buried between the sheets on her bed. She had all but quit housecleaning, and the place was a disaster. I went over one night to dust, do a few loads of laundry. An oversized children's book—the front cover was a painting of an Indian doll in a canoe caught on a wave in the middle of a storm. *Paddle to the Sea.* The waters are white-capped and it looks like the little boat is moving upstream, against the waves. I opened it and skipped through the text, looking mostly at the pictures. It was a story I remembered from school. It is the story of an Indian boy from Canada who longs to have an adventure but can't leave his village. He carves a wooden doll sitting inside a canoe. In the early spring he sets the doll on top of a mountain and waits for the sun to melt the snow. The carved toy takes off for a long journey through and around the Great Lakes, up into Quebec, until finally he makes it out to the sea.

"Is this what this is all about?" I carried the book downstairs to confront my mother.

By this time she was a member of three or four kayak groups. That night she was sitting on the couch, her legs tucked under her, flipping through a new catalog. She rarely drank now. She was convinced that alcohol muddled her concentration. She took a mind-control class at the YWCA in Royal Oak and was convinced that she was smarter. She paid a lot more attention to what she ate, cutting out red meat and fatty foods from her diet. She'd click her tongue at me when I ordered hamburgers or cheese steak sandwiches.

"Excuse me?" she said. She worked out on free weights, and I could see the difference in her shoulders and chest. She was fit. Strong and healthy, she looked much younger than fifty-five.

"This," I said and held up the book. "Is this why you're doing all this kayaking?"

"That's a children's book," she said, and took it from me. "I used to read it to you girls when you were younger."

"No, you didn't," I said. "I never heard this story before."

She bent her head forward and began rubbing the back of her neck. I could hear her joints cracking—her workouts kept her constantly sore. We had installed a shower massage to relax her muscles before bed. She slept less, but it didn't seem to affect her. She was full of energy.

"Mom," I said.

She looked up, her hair covering her face. She no longer had it done every week in the beauty parlor, and now it was an outgrown perm that she cut herself every two or three weeks in the upstairs bathroom. I had just cleaned the sink of hair.

"Okay," she said. "I never read it to you as a kid."

"That's not what I mean," I said, and sat on the armchair across from her. She motioned for me to move. I was sitting on a stack of magazines, but I told her they'd be fine. "You know what I'm talking about."

"It's a book," she said. "That's all."

"It's a book about an Indian who canoes out to the ocean."

"The doll makes it out to the ocean," she explained and opened the book to show me one of the illustrations. "The Indian boy has to stay in his village. Up in Canada."

"And where are you going?" I asked.

"It's almost nine-thirty," she said and pointed to her watch. "I don't think I'll go anywhere tonight."

No one could avoid things better than my mother did. I knew she was planning something and I knew she was soliciting my help, but no matter how many times I asked her to explain, she hesitated and talked about the rapids, the sharp rocks whitewater rafters love but kickers fear. And somewhere in all that avoidance, I became her partner.

It was on our fourth night of camping, just after we had closed the tent and lain down ready and waiting for sleep, when my mother told me she wasn't going to worry about me. It was only eight o'clock, but nightfall comes early in northern Michigan, and it had already been dark for a few hours. We had forgotten candles and used our flashlights only for bathroom visits. Spooked by the quiet woods, we always went together. There was nothing to do but go to bed and wait for morning.

"If you're lonely it's your own fault." My mother's voice was clear in the darkness.

"I guess so," I said. I didn't talk to my mother about my failed relationships. I never told her I was lonely. It was not something I complained about. These were her observations, things she put together about my life. I had spent so much time with her that I had quit thinking about my own problems.

"Life has never made any of us happy," she said. "We don't get that luxury."

"You sound so pessimistic," I said. The sleeping bags had spent the day in the trunk of the car and took a long time to heat up to our body temperatures. My shoulder blades were sore from three nights of sleeping on the frozen ground, and I rolled over onto my stomach. My hipbones bore into the earth and I sat up, wishing I could sleep that way.

"You're alone," she said to me, and though I couldn't see her face, the closed-in tent blocking all light from the spring sky, I knew she was also sitting up, facing me, talking directly to me.

"What about you?" I asked. "Aren't you here with me?" I took my hands out of my sleeping bag and reached out in front of me. I hit her in the face—she was much closer than I expected her to be. She held my fingers up to her lips and kissed them. Her lips were dry and chapped. I could feel the blistering skin and pulled away. We have never been a family who showed much physical affection.

"I want you to be serious," my mother said. "Don't think of this as a joke."

"Isn't that a little like calling the kettle black?" I asked, and because I somehow knew where she was headed, I tried to divert her. "I've been trying to get you to give me a straight answer for the past two years."

"I haven't always known what my answers would be," she said. Her sentences slowed and she got much more serious.

"It's cold, Mom," I said. But by then I was no longer cold. The tent was sealed and the wind had settled for the night. Come morning we would be wet, and then I would remember what it was to be cold.

"I'm ready," she said.

"Are you sure?" I asked.

"I'm feeling strong," she said. "Very strong."

"Is this really what you want to do?"

"Oh, yes," she said. "Yes."

"What if you don't make it?" I asked.

"It's a possibility," she said. "But not the only one."

The night noises outside hummed and we sat quietly and listened for a while.

"Don't go to flea markets," my mother said.

"Excuse me?" I sat up again, and this time I could feel her breath on my face.

"If you're alone and wondering what to do," she said. "Don't waste your time going to flea markets."

"Of course not," I said. "Of course I won't."

"I didn't think so," she said and touched my cheek with the back of her hand.

What Megan and Nina couldn't understand, and what I'm still having a hard time trying to explain to everyone else in the family, was that my mother always anticipated a victorious run. The trip over the falls was to have made her famous. The day was to have ended not in death, but in celebration.

She wanted the victory party to be at the Pier House in Harbor Springs. Halfway between Detroit and the falls, it would be the perfect place for everyone to meet. She was sure the *Detroit Free Press* would pick up the story, after which it might run on syndication, maybe even with a small photograph and a few lines in *People* magazine. She saw herself sitting at the head of a long table, breathlessly explaining to the photographers and newspaper people that she had never been afraid. The conversation would be filled with words like courage, victory, spirit, soul— and for that one moment she might actually be like her beloved basketball stars.

It was to have been glorious. My mother saw her trip over the fifty-foot Tahquamenon Falls not as a stunt or a suicide run but as a quest—something she had searched for, something she wanted—and I could find no reason to stop her. This is not a story of my innocence. I knew exactly what she was doing. But like my mother says, it's all a question of where you're positioning yourself. Even with the roar of the rapids giving you a dry cotton mouth, your hands have to be clenched around the paddle; eyes straight ahead, leg muscles taut, but ready to go. And that's when you lean over, all your weight to one side, and ride straight into your fears.